SHORT SHRIFTS

Confessions of a High School Heretic

Adrian Hart

MINERVA PRESS
MONTREUX   LONDON   WASHINGTON

SHORT SHRIFTS
CONFESSIONS OF A HIGH SCHOOL HERETIC
Copyright © Adrian Hart 1997

ISBN 1 86106 173 0

First published 1997 by
MINERVA PRESS
195 Knightsbridge
London SW7 1RE

Printed in Great Britain by
Arrowhead Books Ltd, Reading, Berkshire

SHORT SHRIFTS
Confessions of a High School Heretic

About the Author

Adrian Hart was born in Sydney in 1971. He was educated at Sydney Adventist High School, then the University of Sydney, where he started writing short stories and poetry. He has worked as a volunteer news reporter with public radio station 2SER-FM, as well as contributing to on-campus publications, *Honi Soit* and *Union Recorder*. Currently, he is undertaking research for a PhD. He lives in Castle Hill and *Short Shrifts* is his first novel.

Author's Note

The following is a work of fiction. None of the characters depicted actually exist. Crookwell High is an imaginary school within an imaginary suburb of an imaginary city which, in a parallel universe, could very well have been Sydney. In particular, Crookwell is not Strathfield, Sandhurst is not Parramatta, Glendale is not Castle Hill, the Sandhurst Sharks is not the Parramatta District Rugby League Football Club, and Jacko is not Peter Sterling, who would never swear on radio. *Home and Away* is very real, however.

Contents

The moment's world, it was; and I was part,
Fleshless and ageless, changeless and made free.

Kenneth Slessor, 'Out of Time'

Prologue

He sits on the bench once the bus has left. He is in no hurry. There will be other buses to the school. They stop here at the station every five minutes. And there are advantages in waiting for the next bus. Now he is at the start of the queue. He will get a choice of seat instead of being forced to stand. The back seat. But he knows that he could have had a seat regardless. He is in Year Twelve now, the senior year. A choice of seat is his privilege. He sighs. It is a privilege that he does not really want.

He takes a worn dollar coin from his pocket. Hard. Milled edging. He feels the dull warmth of it against his skin, the distinctive markings.

He places the coin on his thumb.

There are only two possibilities.

Another approaches and sits on the bench beside him. They know each other. They both wear the uniform of Crookwell High.

"Hi."

"Hi."

"What are you doing?"

"I'm conducting an experiment."

"An experiment?"

"It's a predictive experiment. Based on the laws of probability."

He stares grimly at the coin on his thumb. The other regards the coin too.

Seconds pass.

"What are you predicting?"

He considers the question thoughtfully. Then he takes the coin from his thumb and holds it up so the other can see it more closely. He rotates the surface.

"It only has two sides. Two possibilities."

"So?"

"So it's ideal for predicting two-way outcomes. Life isn't decided for us by a supreme being, you know. Everything that happens is just part of a long sequence of chance actions and reactions. This coin

helps me to predict some of these chance events. Like, say... for instance... I'm going to predict whether the next person who joins this bus queue will be a boy or a girl."

He propels the coin high into the air. It blurs into a transparent sphere, then lands neatly in the palm of his hand. He looks down at the exposed head.

"It's going to be a girl."

"Are you sure?"

"I'm fifty percent certain."

"But you can't use probability like that!"

"Why?"

"Because whatever happens now has nothing to do with the coin."

"But it's a good simulator of real probabilities."

"No it isn't."

"So what do you suggest?"

"Well, for a start, you would need to know how many girls there are at our school who catch the train as compared to the number of boys. Then you would have to weight the probabilities of the outcomes accordingly. For an all-boys school, you'd need a trick coin that always turned up tails."

"I'm glad that I don't go to an all-boys school."

"Why?"

"I don't have a trick coin."

With a snap of his thumb, he tosses the dollar up again. It arcs over his head and into his other hand. Another head.

"I tell you, it's going to be a girl. I'm seventy-five percent certain. The coin never lies."

Another train rumbles away from the station.

"This is a dumb experiment."

He tosses again.

"Another head. That makes me... eighty-seven point five percent sure."

He stops.

"You know, no matter how many times I spin the coin, I'll never be completely sure of the outcome. The chances only increase half as much each time. Maximum."

"I'm not listening."

A crowd of students erupt from the station tunnel. A prefect organises them into a rough queue behind the two Year Twelve students on the bench. They wait in line and fidget and talk to friends they have not seen for six weeks. Another bus will arrive soon.

He is triumphant. A girl stands at the front of the line.

But the other is sceptical.

"That's just luck!"

"Exactly. That's what it's all about. That's life."

"Try it on something else then. I bet that it won't work again."

"Name it."

The other glances around the station, searching for another test subject. Then:

"I know. Predict your HSC result this year."

"My result? But that could be anything. This coin is only a two-way predictor."

"So test whether you will pass or fail then."

He nods approvingly. This is a more interesting proposition.

"Heads you pass..."

"And tails fails. I get the picture."

He places the coin on his thumb once more. A bus turns the corner and approaches. The queue of students bustle behind him. His thumb is tensed – it's a spring-loaded weapon. Sweat breaks out across his face.

"What are you waiting for? The bus is coming."

"I... I think I'll need quite a few tosses to be sure on this one."

"Just toss the coin."

But his thumb refuses to release. The bus pulls up to the stop. The doors open. The queue is restless behind them.

"Toss it!"

In desperation he flicks the dollar into the air. But the launch is skewed, mistimed by the nervous tension in his wrist. Everyone at the bus stop watches its slow upward spiral. Head. Tail. Head. Tail. Head. The coin smacks against the concrete pavement... and rolls along its edge towards the gutter... and falls over the brink... into the drain.

He blinks in astonishment.

"You know what this means?"

The other stands up to get on the bus.

"That your year is what you make of it? That you'll never be sure of what you're going to get in the HSC?"

"Nah. It means that this year is going to be real shit."

He decides to walk to school.

I
TRIALS

ROLLING

What a riot! Total anarchy! Five minutes into the year and already the gloves are off. The fight was started by Billy Loxton of course. He had thrown the first punch at Peter Woolley for winking at him. Something must have happened over the summer holiday break. Greg has spent the morning busily recounting a rumour to everybody that Peter and Sally went all the way at a beach party. I don't believe a word of it. Neither should Billy. Sally is far too good-looking to like Peter. The guy has absolutely nothing going for him.

"Okay, that's enough. Break it up." Richard separates the grapplers and holds them at arm's length.

"You get out of it," snarls Billy. "This is between me and him."

Peter raises an index finger provocatively.

"Right, you bastard..."

And it's on for young and old! Before my eyes, the excess testosterone in Room E3 decide to re-enact the Battle of Agincourt or a finals football fixture: boys race in from all angles to join the fracas, the girls maintain the pretence that nothing is happening and Richard falls under a rain of blows. Jeez! This is getting dangerous! I decide to take evasive action under a desk. This is a perfect opportunity to listen to my new Sony Walkman. I'm not cowardly or anything. I just don't think that the fight has anything to do with me. And it isn't in line with my nihilist philosophy to intervene for some dubious Cause. No, it is far better to stay aloof in these circumstances and let Fate take its fickle course which, after several rather prolonged moments of yelling, punching, kicking and screaming – all intermingled with the riffs of *Dead Bone* – it does.

"Okay Mr Loxton, Peter. Come with me." Deputy Kelly wrenches the two protagonists off the floor by their collars and propels them towards his office. "You can continue your roll call now, Amy," he adds cheerfully as he leaves.

I've really scored it bad this year. Ms Amy French is the most repressed teacher in the school. To have to see her face every morning for roll call is unfortunate. To have her for English as well is downright criminal. I think I might have to lodge a complaint with the School Board. She can't teach, has absolutely no control over the class, and her roll calls, in particular, have no style or panache whatsoever. I know, because I also had her for roll call in Year Eight. It was awful in 8F. Every morning was two minutes of roll call, followed by fifteen minutes of Bible study and prayer for the missionaries in Russia. It could only happen at Crookwell High. The only exception had been the first day, when administrative details bogged her down. Not that she took any time off from prayer, mind. Instead, she chose to ignore the roll call itself. This was probably the best decision she had ever made. After all, who would ever miss the first day of school? It's nothing but a social occasion to meet your friends and haggle over the course syllabus with the teachers. More importantly, there are no assessments due on the second day of school. Why waste a perfectly good undated doctor's certificate?

"Now, where were we? The Ks." Ms French starts reading through the names again. "Gary Kendall?"

"Here." I poke my head up from underneath the desk.

"Oh there you are. William Loxton?"

Silence.

"Ahh, he just left with Mr Kelly," mumbles someone up the front.

"Thank you Greg. Sally McVey?"

"Here."

"Richard Taylor?"

"Yo."

"'Here' or 'Present' will suffice, Richard. Linda Travers?"

"Here."

"Jamie Ulcott?"

"Present."

"And wasn't that Peter Woolley I saw earlier?"

"That's right, Miss. He's now with Mr Kelly too, Miss."

"Thank you Greg." Ms French scribbles a note inside her roll-book.

What is Greg's game? It hasn't taken him long to start licking up his brownie points. Then again, this is the big one; the Higher School Certificate year. In ten months we'll be sitting the final exams. The finals are worth fifty percent of the Tertiary Entrance Rank, that truly beautiful figure which will determine whether I get a place at university or not. The rest of the TER is made up of dodgy school assessments throughout the year, so perhaps Greg's tactic of sucking up to the teachers indicates real nous. Still, I'm not going to sink that low. Well, not yet at any rate. It depends on where I stand going into the trial exams. Until then, I'm going to be a rock.

12F has turned out to be a real mixed bag. On the plus side, it contains the lovely Sally McVey. Richard's here too, and he can be a pretty good bloke when he stops acting the hero in front of everyone. Greg's bearable when he snaps out of his religious mood swings. On the negative side, there's Billy Loxton, who will no doubt become the most renowned export of Crookwell High when he's put away for life in prison. They say he had a brain tumour when he was a kid. I think some crazy doctor must have removed his brain by mistake. Then again, perhaps no one could tell the difference. I suppose that being the son of a church minister doesn't help much. What the hell does Sally see in him? Sure, they both play in the school's First XI cricket team, but he bats and she bowls! Whatever happened to the separate batters' and bowlers' unions? Dad reckons that Typhoon Tyson and Thommo had no time for batsmen. If Sally's going to make a name for herself at the top level, she must do the same. As for the others in the class, well, I don't know them all that much right now, and if I continue to play my cards right, they will remain unknown to me for the rest of the year.

So there we have 12F. A bit rough around the edges, but no better or worse than I had expected. 12C looks to be the place where all the trendy gangs and cliques have been directed, thank goodness. Mr Cooke probably asked for them. He's always had a populist streak. Good riddance to the lot of them. Richard is probably annoyed that Kim Fleming ended up with the intellectuals in 12J. So did Toni Gibson, come to think of it. I don't know why. Obviously, there must be some kind of mistake.

"Gary! Howareyamaaate?"

Then again, Richard probably hasn't realised yet.

"Okay, I guess."

Richard leans over close to whisper in my ear.

"Did you hear? Peter and Sally were porking at the beach party!"

Porking? I look over at Sally to make sure she can't hear what we are talking about. Her beautiful ears were not made for listening to such scurrilous claims.

"You believe that?"

Richard shakes his head.

"Nah. Not really. Greg told me. I'm just having a lend of ya. But I thought you were going to be the one making the moves over the summer break." He jabs a finger in the small of my back. "You were making plans all last year. Sally this, Sally that..."

"Shhhh all right! She'll hear us."

"So what happened?"

I shrug. I *was* going to do something. I had it all worked out. I was the one who was going to express my true feelings for Sally at the beach party, not Peter. But my parents had other ideas. I had been roped into helping them build a holiday shack in an obscure country retreat one hundred and fifty kilometres away. I had tried to explain to Dad my lack of skill with the hammer and saw, but he had just said 'all the more reason to give you some practice' or some such pragmatic nonsense. So was it my fault when an overhead beam I nailed fell down on his shoulder? Was it my fault that I didn't use the right nails? Was it?

"So?"

"Look Richard. I just never had the opportunity. Not all of us get to spend the summer break on the beach, you know..."

But before I can develop my argument further, I am interrupted by Ms French who, in her last duty for this morning's roll call, distributes the school's annual events calendar. I snatch at one greedily. It is bad enough that Sally is still going with Billy, but a rumour that the heir apparent is Peter Woolley is even more distressing. Heck, I need some good news, and if last year's calendar is anything to go by... Yep, sure enough, the first unofficial holiday of the year is only twenty-three days away: swimming carnival.

TALENT

Whoever said that god doesn't distribute talent equally is plain wrong – she doesn't exist. But whoever or whatever *does* do the distributing never got around to reading Rosseau's *Dissertation on Inequality*. Or at least couldn't read French and didn't know where to find an English translation. Or, like me, found that the computerised catalogues at the local library listed the translation as 'in process' for three years, and 'missing' for the last two.

I love school sporting carnivals and not only because they're always rostered on school days. Well, that's an added benefit, but it's mainly my only chance to observe the physiques of some of the more attractive girls in the school. It's hard to catch them out of their 'sacks' – dubious strips of blue-grey material which pass as school uniform. Swimming carnivals can put a warm glow in even the smallest of Speedo briefs. I'll never forget the stunning lycra number that Sally wore last year. Neither will the vocal male contingent from 10R who had taken up a section of the stand behind me. Of course, I'm not much of a swimmer myself. Only those with good bods should take to the water. My delicate frame doesn't hit it off all that well with a pair of Speedos. In fact, I gave up the paddling caper in Grade Three when Carol Lee giggled at the shape residing in my tight swimmers. That wangers tend to shrink in cold water is an unfortunate aspect of masculinity.

So I turned to athletics and running. After all, I had reasoned to myself, I come from a pedigree sporting family – my older sister still holds school age records today. Jeez! What I could say about Sarah! She really took school sport seriously. I think she was the last student at Crookwell High who actually took her Sundays off to train at our local oval in Glendale. Other competitors would shrivel in despair when Sarah turned up with her own blocks and spikes at the start of the one hundred metre heats. It may have been just a generational thing, but she always liked to be fully equipped. I remember that day several years back when Dad refused to buy her an Olympics-approved complete hurdling set. She took it pretty hard. But sometimes these things can get out of hand and, anyway, it just wouldn't all fit in the boot of the car that easily.

That was also the year I left Glendale Primary to enter the big league of high school competitive sport.

"Hey, it's another Kendall!" Danny 'Rocket' Blackstone had said when my name was put up during the Sports House roll call. He was the star sprinter in Year Twelve and held the suspect position of House Captain. He strode up to me and shook my hand vigorously. "Great to have you aboard, mate."

"I'm not really that good." I had felt a bit embarrassed by the attention.

"Ha. That's what Sarah said just before she broke the state record in the fifteen hundred!" He chuckled and patted my shoulder before wandering off to hassle some other new kid.

At the time I was dumb enough to believe the bullshit he was tossing my way. After all, I *had* finished third in primary school for the 'under-twelves' fifty metres. That there were only three boys in the 'under-twelve' bracket at Glendale Primary didn't quite enter my calculations. Nor did the fact that Jerome Miles, one of the select trio, had been replaced at the last moment by his kid brother, Simon, due to a sudden attack of meningitis.

These thoughts only began to trouble me when I lined up for my first race. At Primary, I had been used to having plenty of empty lanes to trot about in, but lined up against me now were no less than seven other hopefuls, all with ambitiously blank faces transfixed upon the tape one hundred metres away. One hundred metres! What had happened to my speciality – the fifty metre canter? Who had made the distance twice as long? How come all the other racers looked twice my height? And why did they have to pull a tape across the finish line? The pace I travelled never necessitated such a device. But the starter raised his gun and these thoughts raced from my mind, not even getting pulled up by the race officials for a false start.

I think I made the right decision by collapsing on my left knee three seconds into the sprint. I was in lane four. Lanes one to three were already streaking away from me at breakneck speed by the time I faked a torn medial ligament. By the time I hit the ground, lanes five to eight were almost through the tape. It really was the only way out of an embarrassing situation, although the school doctor became a trifle annoyed after he helped stretcher me all the way to sick bay.

I hadn't fooled the students either.

"You didn't do your knee," Rocket said afterwards.

"Oh?" I contended, proudly exhibiting the fresh swaddling around my left leg.

"Usually the injured person doesn't help by fetching the stretcher. You should have stayed down."

"Ah."

At that point I knew that athletics wasn't my game. I think Rocket knew it too. He shook his head and walked off to rejoin the House cheergirls. They laughed at something he said before heading off to the sandpit to observe the long-jumpers. I lay back down on the bed and had a long think. It's always a bit of a letdown when you learn that you're no longer the best at something or, in my case, third-best. I knew that I didn't have the talent to be a class athlete. Sure, training could help, but training could only push me so far. It would take years before I could become competitive in any way. But there was more to life than mere athletic prowess. I was a thinker. I would concentrate on my studies and use my talent to win academic prizes in my final year of high school. And one day that might become a fair reason for girls to go out with me instead of with jocks like Rocket. Yep, that day in Year Seven I discovered that everyone had their own, unique talent. Mine was in intellectual pursuits, Rocket's was in sprints and the world was just great.

Then Rocket became Dux and pissed me right off.

PUNISHMENT

There is no justice in the world.

Peter Woolley has been expelled and Billy Loxton remains to harass and maim more members of the student body. Something smells really fishy here. Could it be that Billy was spared because of his father's religious connections with the school? Has a dodgy deal been struck? Poor old Pete. I don't know him all that much. Nobody does. But I'm sure that he must be a halfway decent bloke to give Billy the finger in the way he did. That took real guts. His parents probably aren't high up in the church. If they were, he might still be here too. Bloody School Board. It's a right nasty piece of work – completely totalitarian and answerable to no one. Someone will have to be elected to institute some real democratic safeguards in the future. I was not asked once to provide my eye-witness, under-the-table evidence of the incident.

Crookwell High's 'corrective' policy operates on four levels, according to the severity of the crime. The worst crimes attract the gravest possible punishment – expulsion, the capital punishment of the schooling system. Expelled students never come back (except to torch the science buildings on the odd occasion). Offences falling within this category include fighting, smoking, drinking alcoholic beverages in the school grounds, drinking alcoholic beverages outside the school grounds, being convicted of any offence outside school, vandalism of school property, wearing any kind of earlobe ornamentation, engaging in loving gestures with the opposite sex, engaging in loving gestures with the same sex, engaging in loving gestures with yourself in the locker rooms, preaching the non-existence of god (this *is* a religious school), swearing (at teachers or other members of staff), wagging classes, or possessing items of a pornographic nature. Of course, expulsion (like capital punishment) doesn't solve the problem – it simply moves it on to another school.

One level short of capital punishment is the lengthy jail sentence: suspension. Generally, the offences here include those from the expulsion category (for first-time offenders) plus a few less serious ones: not wearing proper school uniform (this includes make-up and jewellery), chewing gum in class, touching the opposite sex for any reason, touching the same sex for a violent reason (touching the same sex for a sexual reason invites expulsion), professing a belief that there will be no second coming of Christ, swearing (at other students), wagging Bible class, or possessing items of 'soft' pornography, such as *Cleo* or other girlie magazines. The length of the sentence can also be used as a method of differentiating the severity of the crime. Suspensions at Crookwell High generally last between one and four weeks. During this time, the convicted felon lives a life of luxury at home – sleeping, catching up on movies from the video store, sunbaking on the beach et cetera – whilst decent folk are forced to attend school and sit HSC assessments. Sometimes I wonder who, exactly, is serving time.

Another level down again are lunchtime detentions. Basically, these are community service obligations. Crookwell High seems to have a never-ending list of jobs and maintenance tasks that need to be performed each week, and rallying a pliant underage workforce is easy enough. Every year, some students turn against their brothers and sisters and become agents for the incumbent authority, Deputy Kelly. Known colloquially as 'prefects', these students feed their growing megalomania by writing detention slips to anyone who upsets them. The innocent victims of their insecurities and paranoias are then forced to clean toilets, weed lawns, wipe windows, scrape the rust off the school gates, carry heavy building materials to anywhere, and back again, catalogue library books and polish the floor of the basketball court. It is rumoured that the school cannot afford a regular cleaner, and thus that the prefects operate on a quota system so that all the jobs get done. I can only agree. So far, the only year that I managed to escape lunchtime detention was Year Eight, a period when the head prefect was trying to crack on to my older sister. Prefects enter the police force as soon as they finish school.

Finally, for the very pettiest of offences, Crookwell High has introduced a demerit system. It is quite unique. Every student has a DQ (demerit quotient) placed on their student record. Demerits are the parking fines of the punishment regime: they are an inconvenience if anything, and nobody takes them seriously. Sure, speaking rudely to a prefect, being late for class, or having one's shirt half out costs several demerit points, but who really gives a stuff? It takes about twenty demerit points before the community service slips start coming in. Furthermore, in line with the moral nature of the school, it is possible to remove demerits from one's record via appropriate 'good deeds'. I'm not entirely sure what constitutes a 'good deed'. Hopefully, I'll never have to find out. Last year, Greg had some merits installed on his DQ and ended the season with a small surplus. He could have spent the last day of Year Eleven with his shirt out. He could have called no less than three prefects total arseholes. But he didn't want to spoil his perfect record.

"So why did Peter get chucked out?" asks Kim during the regular lunchtime chat session on the field. Five of us lie on the grass catching the afternoon sun: Richard, Kim, Toni, Greg and myself. The question troubles all of us.

"Didn't you hear? Sally and Peter did the business..."

"Bullshit Greg." Richard is not in the mood for nonsense this time. "Man! You speak a lot of shit sometimes. Sally's not like that."

"But it's true!"

"Yeah, sure Greg."

"How come you guys never believe me?"

"It's unfair that Billy isn't at least on suspension," says Kim. "He's always fighting."

I give my own shrift.

"I think it has something to do with the fact that Billy's dad is a church minister at Rundle. That guy's probably responsible for half the student population being here. He has a lot of power."

Kim seems to share my feelings. She, Toni and myself are all the product of the Glendale branch of the church, although I've now lost whatever spiritual conviction my primary school had given me. So have my parents. I used to wonder why they keep insisting that I attend Crookwell High. I reckon it's because they get a large education discount for still claiming to be religious. Crookwell High is the only high school in the area affiliated to the church, so it attracts a mix of students from both Glendale and Rundle. Us Glendallians have always been keen rivals of the Rundler denomination, and when the opposition consists of social blemishes like Billy 'Mad Dog' Loxton and clique queen Jennifer Dukes, it's not hard to maintain that rivalry. Greg's a bit of an exception. He's from Rundle, but he keeps a foot in both camps. He probably considers himself a peace-maker. If so, he hasn't achieved very much. Even now, in Year Twelve, I still view anyone from the Rundle church as a bit of a drop-kick, Greg included. Old habits die hard.

But Toni disagrees with my theory.

"Probably Peter just left, you know..."

"On the first day?" It sounds a little far-fetched to me.

"Well let's face it. This school isn't renowned for its quality of education. Perhaps he just got accepted into a better school like Huxley or Tresham and decided to go out with a bang. Remember Stephen?"

Yeah, fair call, I guess. Stephen Saunders used to be in our year, but he left in Year Nine for Tresham College, an esteemed private school in the city. Never heard from him since. He didn't really want to go, but I think his parents knew that staying here would be deleterious for his HSC chances. Crookwell High is more concerned about churning out missionaries than high HSC results. The School Board never bothers to look in the Top 1000 which is published in the newspapers each year. They are only concerned about how many students will go on to attend the religiously-affiliated Harvey College. And anyway, Peter *is* a mysterious character. Who knows what is going on inside that head of his? Well, I know he holds no particular love in his heart for Crookwell High. He never really spoke to anyone. Ever. Sometimes I think he holds us all in contempt. In fact, I'm sure he does. But then again, there's a lot at Crookwell High to be contemptuous about. If Toni's theory is correct, well, good luck to him. I admire his stance. I only wish that more of us could have escape routes from this educational void.

The first of this year's HSC assessments is just ten days away, and, being in this school, that is punishment enough.

JESUS!

Ten days is a lifetime in some respects. I've learned a lot of things. Firstly, Toni was right in saying that Peter had been accepted into another school, although I'm not sure if that happened before or after the episode with Billy and Deputy Kelly. I saw Peter yesterday on my home railway station, Sandhurst, wearing a Tresham school uniform. I can't figure him out – he looked even more disgruntled with life than before. Secondly, Sally has been upset about something all week and pulled out of racing at the swimming carnival. I wasn't going anyway, so no change of schedule there. Thirdly, I've learned that ten days – although a lifetime – is not quite enough time to write an assessed Economics essay on micro-economic reform. It's due next period and I have still to refute the so-called inefficiencies of the ports, damn privatisation, lend support to a centralised wages policy, and critique the deregulation of the financial sector. Hopefully I'll have it all finished by the end of Bible.

"Now, Mr Kendall, what are you doing?"

I look up into the cold grey eyes of Old Ronny Wright: Bible teacher, school chaplain and careers representative for Harvey College. There is no point covering my work.

"That's not Bible is it?" he notes, shaking his head in his usual condescending manner. Give the man a cigar! "Gary, the class was discussing the eternal life offered to us by Jesus. Would you care to give us your view?"

"Jesus!" I have an assessed essay, worth at least five percent of my final HSC mark for Economics, due next period and Old Ron wants me to share my atheism with the rest of the class? Give me a break!

"Yes, that's right. Jesus."

Jesus? Well, personally, I feel for the guy. I really do.

I imagine that he was just your everyday political revolutionary from Nazareth (a radical haven by all accounts), trying his best to protest against the Roman imperialist lackeys who occupied his homelands.

How the hell he got caught up with religion and eternal life is anyone's guess. Jesus is a pretty common name, too. At least it was a common name – and still is a common name in some countries. But to call your kid Jesus here is likely to upset your Christian neighbours. Anyway, the name was probably as popular as Jason is today, yet no one I know of is spinning a religion around any Jason who protests against American foreign policy. Probably I just have to wait another couple of hundred years for it to take off. Yet some people I know consider that the very existence of Jesus proves the existence of god. This would probably be news to Jesus, if he had lived long enough to see what a personality cult had developed around his surname.

"Jesus can't give us eternal life. He's dead." What else can I say? I can't lie about this. I need to get back to my Economics essay. However, my somewhat succinct summation draws twitters from 12F and palpable angst from Greg.

"But He is alive!"

Oh god. I thrust my pen down in exasperation. Yeah, I know the story. The Romans, taking exception to the snotty-nosed upstart, and probably alarmed at how much popular support he has with his folks, decide that the only good Jesus is a dead Jesus. So they arrest him, give him a quick mock trial, satisfy a few outspoken reactionaries by releasing a tax cheat from prison in his place, and string him up on the latest capital punishment gadgetry. There, no more problems. But they hadn't counted on the imagination of Jesus' comrades or the sheer gullibility of his followers. Mark, Matty, Luke, John and Paul were not content with their little bit of revolution coming to a premature end. They were raking it in at the synagogues. The show had to go on. I can picture the scene now in my head:

Matty: Hang on. Did anyone see that he was dead?

Luke: *(Glumly)* Only the whole bloody city. We're ruined.

Matty: We couldn't say that he was holding his breath?

Luke: For two days?

Paul: Guys, guys! I've got it! We grab Jesus' body and bury it somewhere in the wilderness. Then, when mourners come to visit the tomb, we all jump out from behind some juniper bushes and say that he rose from the dead.

John: *(After a period of awkward silence)* But where will he be, Paul?

Paul: Uh, I don't know. He just keeps rising, I guess. Goes to heaven or something. Mary will go along with it too. She needs the cash.

Luke: *(Whiningly)* But what if people say that we're full of crap?

Mark: We'll write it all down. I'm pretty nifty with the stylus. Perhaps you guys could write Jesus' story too.

John: We'd better get together to make sure we are writing the same stuff. The story has to be consistent or no one will believe us.

Paul: On that point, perhaps it would give us the sympathy vote in the future if Barabbas was a murderer or something, instead of only failing to lodge his tax returns on time. I've got a hunch the difference will matter in a couple of millennia.

Matty: Damn straight, Paul. And we'll organise copies to put in some pottery jars by the Dead Sea for future archaeologists to stumble across. They'll believe anything that's old.

And so a religion is spawned. I could speak up, but Greg wouldn't believe me. Nor would Old Ronny. And, as much as I'd like to, I just couldn't recount to the class the Gospel according to Gary Kendall, could I? Ronny would send me up to Deputy Kelly for a private chat about being rude and insubordinate – and basically treating Bible class with the contempt it deserves. I've heard that the New Testament has all been plagiarised from the Koran anyway. But at Crookwell High this is *evil* talk; talk from the devil himself. Is it evil, though, to have your doubts about a story where the main character is born to a virgin, feeds the five thousand with a couple of loaves of bread and some fish fingers (what were they smoking back then?), gives Lazurus a second chance at life, dies by crucifixion, reappears three days later on a hilltop with only his comrades to verify the story (surprise surprise), and finally floats off into space without a space-suit? Yeah. Right. In a few hundred years, people will look back on Christianity as a really bizarre, primitive belief system, much like we tend to view the sacred beliefs of Australian Aborigines or ancient Egyptians.

"Well Gary, we're all waiting..."

I could be silent or crude, but I don't want this interruption to continue. Better just to play along.

"Yes, sorry. Of course Jesus is alive. Hallelujah." And he plays halfback for the Sandhurst Sharks.

Ronny smiles. The man just doesn't understand sarcasm.

"Thank you Gary." He moves off from my table and returns to the blackboard. "And He died for all of us, to offer us a choice, before rising again on the third day. He has given us the choice of entering the Kingdom of Heaven. He has offered us eternal life with Him. You know, I think that Heaven will be a really great place. Only the best things will happen there..."

What? Now that I *must* contest.

Anyone who's been on an overnight excursion in a co-ed school knows that the best things happen right here on Earth – in sleeping bags.

BAGGED

Some of the best things happen in sleeping bags.

Regardless of the impossibility of defining an absolute truth (and the impossibility of accepting the truth of this impossibility), I can nonetheless get away with this crude generalisation based upon some extracurricular experiences I had last year. During this trying period of my existence I had suffered from a particularly common teenage male malady – lack of sex. I still do, come to think of it. But it seemed to hurt me more last year. I couldn't understand what I was doing wrong. I wasn't the ugliest kid in class, nor the brightest, for both are inevitably doomed to failure on this score. Now I reckon it's because I'm just hopelessly average. I have enough spots on my face to disfigure my looks, yet not enough to be the centre of attention. I always play the fool in English drama, never Hamlet or Macbeth. I'm just a tag-along, a hanger-onner.

But hell, the puritanism of the school teaching staff and administration doesn't help. Talking to the opposite gender is seen as a flagrant breach of the Gospel according to St Paul. Holding hands or any other physical contact will send you straight to hell via Deputy Kelly's office, without even a King James concordance to pass the time. It's getting so bad now that even the most routine love letters are being signed 'Anon.', a development which, to be frank, has led to some most awkward mix-ups, as well as a high degree of bemusement amongst the inexperienced.

Of course, the more rebellious youths flout the rules occasionally. Clandestine meetings are arranged under the stairwell. Passionate kisses can be heard coming from the small office between the Geography and Economics rooms during lunchtime. Serious bouts of heavy petting are popular in the photography darkroom. The student body is a heaving, tumbling, rampant mass of sexual passion; a cornucopia of lust, love and desire which is impossible to regulate completely. And, for the ardent sexual revolutionary, no better opportunity presents itself than on the intermittent weekend excursions sponsored by the school in the name of 'extracurricular education'.

Yes, I knew what these excursions were *really* for, even if the teachers did not. So, having finished the first round of HSC assessments in the second semester of Year Eleven, I had felt due for a little release from the stress and tension. Unfortunately, I did not have much of a choice in the trips. On offer was a cycling expedition, a weekend of prayer at Harvey College, caving in the highlands, or a week in the country on tour with the school's First XI cricketers. Of course, only one ready to risk life and limb for a chance with Sally McVey would go on more than one of these trips. But the odds had seemingly grown in my favour, I thought. Sally and Billy had been going through a 'rough patch'. (Billy had apparently made a pass at clique queen, Jennifer Dukes.) It was the perfect time to take a risk, before more HSC assessments snowballed upon me.

So I chose all four.

Perhaps, on reflection, the greatest mistake was the cycling trip. The teacher in charge, Mr Robertson from metalwork, was surprised to learn that I was a keen cyclist but I had informed him that I often cycled to the newsagent and back again on my trusty Malvern Star, and my gear changes up the steep incline of Edward Street were quite deft. I had even bought a new cycling computer. With Sally already signed up for the trip, I probably exaggerated my skills a little, but heck, it was going to be worth it. I packed a rather large sleeping bag for the ride – Sally was taller than me and I thought that, if the best came to the best, I would need the extra manoeuvring space. Dad gave me a lift to Crookwell and I rode the final few hundred metres to the school gates, so as not to tire myself out too early. It was a very wobbly ride. The sleeping bag jutted out from under my saddle like a large, green sausage roll.

"So where's Sally?" I had asked once we were underway, somewhere between Crookwell and North Crookwell. Mr Robertson produced a blank expression.

"Sally?" Then his features relaxed knowingly. "Oh, Sally McVey. Yeah, uh, she had to pull out. She couldn't make it."

"What?"

"You know, Gary, we're in for a great trip. Clear weather all the way, I hear."

I gripped the handlebars tightly. My flashy odometer skipped over to 00003. Two hundred kilometres into the journey, Mr Robertson joined me in my sleeping bag. His bag had allegedly ripped apart, courtesy of a worn catch on his right pannier bag. That cycling trip proved very long and arduous.

Ditto for the caving. It was just my luck that Mr Robertson was also an expert pot-holer.

Trips to Harvey College, on the other hand, are more educational, or so I was led to believe. The College is the church's alternative to a decent university education. Set in the mountains near Bradden Hill, it is the go-between that places graduates of Crookwell High closer to god. Students are taught about sin, the approaching second coming of Christ cum nuclear Armageddon as foretold by the resident (though dead) prophet, Amelia Cuthbert, and how to diversify industrial share portfolios against unsystematic risk. Every year, the leaving class of the high school is invited up into the high country to savour a Harvey education, supplemented by a diet of Weetbix and vegelinks from the College's cafeteria.

But my biggest thrills were reserved for a secretive late night rendezvous at the swing bridge which spanned a mosquito-infested creek at the rear of the campus. I had joshed and joked around with Richard enough until he agreed to ask Kim to ask Toni to ask Linda to ask Sally to join us by the bridge after curfew.

"What about the mossies?" Kim had asked.

"We'll go down in our sleeping bags," I suggested.

And, curiously enough, this was considered an ingenious plan by the others. So, enrobed in our regimental khaki-green camouflage body-sheaths, we had crept through the patrolled dormitories and hopped our way down the dirt track to the bridge. I must admit to feeling surprised, though pleased, when Sally turned up. She knew that Richard and I were the only guys there, and she had come!

Now, there isn't much you can do late at night in a religious institution with attractive girls on a swing bridge, so it wasn't too long before I had produced the pack of cards for the obligatory game of strip poker. On the hard wooden bridge we sat: dealing cards, laughing, producing articles of clothing from within our sleeping bags, and pulling the zippers of the bags closer to our necks. As the game progressed, I discovered that my desire in witnessing Sally *sans brassiere* was slowly, but surely, being matched by my own fear of being exposed. Disquieting thoughts prodded my subconscious, like: why would Sally wish to see my thin naked body when she could have the muscular Billy Loxton every other day of the week? Come to think of it, where was

Billy? Why did Sally wear thirty-two hair ribbons? Why did I come wearing only three items of clothing? Why was my zipper stuck half-way up my bag?

I was completely naked (and Sally almost out of hair-ribbons) by the time the teachers arrived to break up our pagan fertility ritual. Sally, Kim and Toni raced screaming into the grove of trees along the bank of the creek. Richard pulled the hood of his sleeping bag over his head and made like a rock. That my own efforts to escape were thwarted by Mr Robertson came as a further blow.

I made doubly sure that Mr Robertson was not on the list for the cricket tour the following week. I'm not a cricketer myself. In fact, like swimming, I gave up the game early in the piece to become a nihilist existentialist. But Sally had been in exceptional form that year. I think she is the only girl from our school to tour with the First XI. I think that's why I like her so much: she is a driving force for equality between the sexes. Of course, she's pretty sexy and I admire that too. So I had decided to tag along in my capacity as philosophical fan and optimistic lover.

The match had taken place at Swinton High School, and our team was housed inside the school gymnasium. The night grew cold – typical for early spring in the country – and the teachers retired to a small classroom where they shared a heater. We were left to sort our sleeping bags into neat rows and columns on the basketball court. I made sure that my bag was not too far from Sally's. The day had been a great success, despite Crookwell losing its first game. In particular, Billy Loxton had been hit on the head by a rather vicious delivery from Tyron Trotter, Swinton's answer to Harold Larwood, and was sleeping the injury off in sick bay.

Sally was alone. I could hardly believe my luck. That she was alone amongst twenty-seven sex-starved male cricketers didn't really occur to me until after I crept to where she lay, straddled over the three-point line of the basketball court.

Richard looked up at me with a startled yelp as I lowered the zipper. "Shit! I thought you were Miss French."

I eyed him disapprovingly. I was not Ms French, that was certain. What was less certain was what Richard, my best buddy, was doing in Sally's sleeping bag. My mouth hung agape.

"Bugger off Gary," suggested Sally, poking her head up. "And if you tell Billy I'll bash your head in."

And so bugger off I did, back to my own rude sleeping quarters. The tangle of relationships within a school can be most confusing sometimes. I never knew that Sally and Richard were hitting it off. I thought Richard was going with Kim. Billy probably didn't know either. But by the look of his head after the bouncer, he wasn't going to know much for a long time yet.

I couldn't sleep that night. I pulled the zipper of my sleeping bag right up to my Adam's apple, wishing I could have done the same on the swing bridge at Harvey College. That Richard Taylor! I knew then why Sally had turned up. I had been so naive. I thought of Sally and Richard and Billy and Kim and even Mr Robertson. I rolled over and scrunched myself up into a ball. But Sally just wouldn't get out of my mind, so, rather than wasting the precious thoughts, I masturbated myself to an absolutely glorious orgasm.

Then I fell into a deep, peaceful sleep.

You know, contrary to popular opinion, some of the best things do happen right here on Earth – in sleeping bags.

DUPES

I've known Richard Taylor for three years now. He turned up at Crookwell in Year Nine from Huxley High. It was sickening, at first, to see the girls go absolutely crazy over him.

"The new guy's in my maths class," one had drooled by the bubblers.

"That's nothing," another would reply. "I've got him in PE. God, you should see him in a tee-shirt and a tight pair of shorts. What a bod! What a hunk!"

I had nearly vomited up my eggplant sandwich. What is it about new guys in the school that make them so attractive to girls? It's probably the fact that the girls don't know the first bloody thing about them. Richard *could* have been a mass murderer or rapist. He *could* have been a violent mental patient on day release from an institution. He *could* have been gay. Not that there's anything wrong with being gay, but it sure would have been a major stumbling block for at least some of the girls in my year. Girls don't think about the sorts of risks they take in their relationships. They just go for anyone halfway attractive who holds a bit of mystique. This allows them to fantasise about what their target could be: sensitive, honest, good in bed, in possession of a big wanger and so on. It's not surprising that so many of them are hurt, or let down, or both. But then they have the nerve to turn around and say that *guys* think with their dicks. Talk about being hypocritical! If anyone should be charged of thinking with their dicks, it's girls. Well, thinking with whatever they have underneath their skirts at any rate. Girls are so easily duped when it comes to assessing the opposite sex.

From the very first moment I saw Richard, I had felt that it was my duty to warn Sally about the danger. I knew her game. I had seen her gazing in Richard's direction during Music when her attention should have been firmly fixed upon Ms Kennedy's glockenspiel.

"Oh nick off, Gary. I'm trying to study for the Bible test in sixth period." She revealed some notes she had smuggled underneath the table, between her smooth, brown legs. I had to admit to myself, even in Year Nine, that Sally had nice legs.

"I said nick off!"

But why study Bible? How could anyone think about that religious twaddle when there were more pressing concerns to be worried about?

"Sally. I know that you're interested in the new guy, but I don't trust him. He's just too good looking for his own good. He must be hiding something."

Sally shrugged. "Who cares? Just leave me alone will ya?"

"But it's for your own good!"

"Look Gary. I don't need you to look after me. If you're so concerned, why don't you try to find something out about him instead of hassling me?"

It was a good idea, really. Both Richard and I had PE after Music. Normally I took as long as possible to change into my tight yellow tee-shirt, black shorts and white Dunlop sneakers. The gear made me look as thin as those starving Africans on the aid advertisements on telly. The less time I spent in them, the better. Not only that, but Mr Pollard had the class on another one of those stupid American-style fitness routines. Over the forty-five minute period one had to perform shuttle runs, standing broad jumps, standing high jumps, back extension exercises, sit-ups and the like. It was bloody intolerable. But this time it was different. This time I had a mission to perform: Operation Observe the New Kid and Report Back to Sally. I raced into the gym hall and set up my covert operations by the wall-climbing exercise, keeping my eyes peeled for Richard. It shouldn't have been too hard to locate him. All I had to do was follow the eyes of the girls. Still, they weren't out of the change-rooms. I decided to practice on the wall-climbing apparatus so as to look more inconspicuous. After a few moments of fumbling and stretching, I heard a voice behind me.

"You're doing it wrong, you know."

I wheeled around to face my accuser, still hanging by the metal wall pegs. It was Billy Loxton, and he didn't look very happy. Even in Year Nine he had a body that most grown men would have been proud of, and a round shaved head that a neo-Nazi would have died for. "You should be using your arms more," he muttered. Then he wrenched me from the wall quite violently. I landed on my chest, the wind knocked out of me. Billy picked me up by my hair and relocated my face into the brick wall, his weight firmly pressed against my back. "My mates reckon you've been talking to Sally in Music..."

"But... but..."

"Keep your eyes off Sally, you turd. Don't look at her. Don't talk to her. Don't even *exist* in the same room as her. You got that?"

I wheezed in agreement. Sure thing, Billy, mate. Where had all the air gone?

"If I see you near her again, I'll..."

Then a different voice. Mocking.

"Well hey! I didn't know that this school was so *open* about homosexuality."

Billy looked up, surprised. I must admit that I was a little shocked myself. Certainly, Billy and I were locked in a somewhat ambiguous position, but no one at school ever called Billy a homo and stayed in one piece. Richard did both.

"Get lost, new kid," snarled Billy.

"Get lost! Oh my. Don't they teach you to swear properly at this school, you fucker? Now why don't you just run along and fuck yourself, instead of this guy?"

Billy hesitated, testing the strength of the challenge, then dropped me back down on to the floor. "You're dead," was all he whispered as he brushed past Richard and drifted to the standing long-jump.

That was hardly how I had expected my surveillance assignment to pan out. It was bad enough having Billy in my face (or, more precisely, on my back – my face had been in the wall), but to be rescued by Richard was more than I could bear. I was a man, damn it. I could look after myself. So what if I got beat up? It was a far better thing to be beaten up in a fair fight than to win by sheer weight of numbers.

"Shit. I'm sorry, man," said Richard once I had regathered my breath and explained my predicament. "If it's any consolation, no one saw it. I guess I just lost myself for a moment. Thought I was back at my old school."

I pursed my lips. "Oh, just forget it, all right? If I need a hand in the future, I'll ask for it." Richard shrugged and pulled up his Sandhurst football socks. *Sandhurst* socks? Then I was the one who lost myself. "You support *Sandhurst?*" I was incredulous. Only those possessing the worst kind of bad taste would be seen in Sandhurst gear at Crookwell. To support Sandhurst made you the ultimate loser. The school really was a Rundle safehaven. Even students from Glendale – a suburb right next to Sandhurst for Christ's sake! – were too ashamed of the Sharks' recent win-loss record to support them in public. Well, *nearly* everyone. There was one desperate kid who had possessed the required self-loathing in the past to don the Sandhurst colours. Me.

"Jacko?"

"Legend."

"Smithy?"

"Dead-set legend."

"The King?"

"Genius."

Richard and I exchanged superlatives to describe each and every player of the premier (though, unfortunately, eleventh-placed) football team in the competition. The previous five years had been a real struggle for us die-hard Sandhurst fans. Both Richard and I were at a loss to explain why the Sharks had missed the finals for so long. It was not as though the club had no money to buy decent players. The Sharks were doing very well financially. The whole area was upper-middle class.

"They just can't keep their good up-and-coming youngsters," I quipped.

"Or attract the top players from other clubs," said Richard. "Once the losing mentality becomes entrenched, it's hard to turn the club around. Man, the management has a lot to answer for. We used to have a winning team."

And you know what? All up, the new guy wasn't as bad as many people in the school had made him out to be. We talked throughout that PE class about many things. He told me about the terrible times he'd had at his old school. I told him about all the terrible times I'd had at Crookwell High. He told me, sadly, that he lived in Sandhurst. I told him, equally sadly, that he was not alone in his bourgeois roots. I came from the district myself – a particularly nasty side of Glendale that was just as upwardly mobile. He asked about the girls in the school. I explained, as best I could, the current Who's Going With Whom scenarios: Sally and Billy were an item, much to my disgust; ditto for Lisa and Ben, Tanya and Grant, Chrissy and Mark, Elyse and Warwick, Rita and David, or was that Lisa with David and Rita with Ben...?

"Who's that by the door?" interrupted Richard.

I glanced over to see Toni and Kim looking our way.

"The one on the right is Toni Gibson. She's a real rager. Always up to date on the trends and fashions. The shorter one on the left is Kim..."

"She's cute."

"Uh yeah. You think so?"

"I know so."

And so, in this vomitingly sick-sweet way, Richard and Kim embarked upon a steady relationship which has lasted ever since. Yes, despite Billy's threat, Richard has lived a remarkably full and satisfying life at Crookwell High. He certainly had me fooled. Duped even. It had been quite a shock to discover him in Sally's sleeping bag last year. They had both sworn me to secrecy of course. The day following the bagging fiasco, Richard told me that it was only a passing fling. He reckoned that Sally didn't like him as much after what he did that night. He said that he was still going to go with Kim when we got back to Crookwell. Jeez! I couldn't believe it. What kind of guy cheats on his gal from school? What kind of guy sleeps around with such ease? What kind of guy gets into a sleeping bag with Sally McVey in a crowded hall while Billy 'Mad Dog' Loxton is sleeping off a Tyron Trotter bouncer in sick-bay?

Richard Taylor.

Why can't I be more like him?

VOTE

It's that time of the year again when we students have to elect representatives for the School Council. These young, dynamic leaders will be our voice in the helter-skelter of Crookwell High's boardroom politics. They will stand up for our rights on the important issues: whether we'll be able to buy chocolate from the school canteen, how changes will be made to the detention/demerit system, where we will spend our annual school excursion, and whether it is a mortal sin to watch television on the Sabbath.

Yeah, I don't really give a rat's arse about the elections. Generally, I just vote for any turd or moron. Just like real political elections so I hear. I can't wait to get the vote.

"But you've got to vote *properly*," says Greg.

Why? School Council elections have to be the most stupid and irrelevant events on the student calendar, apart from parent-teacher nights and exams. Especially at Crookwell High. Students don't get any real power at our school. They are a minority on the Board even when they are allowed into the room to debate motions. As if the Principal or the Deputy will allow any diminution of their power. If they intend to, then why don't they go the whole hog? Why not let the students run the school themselves? I've read quite a lot about libertarian schools in the paper recently while cutting out business articles for my Economics scrapbook. Apparently, these libertarian experiments usually degenerate into orgies of class-skipping, sex, and total anarchy. Sounds like fun. American libertarians aren't too concerned though. They say it promotes responsibility for decision-making and instills self-discipline. I'm not too sure about that. Regardless, I can't see the church sanctioning the freedom to live without their sanctions. Moral standards would certainly fall, concerned upright (and uptight) parents would complain and the staff would be out on their collective ear for sure. God would probably disagree too. After all, she doesn't give us the power to choose our lifestyle. Follow me or miss out on eternal life. In fact, why don't you go to hell? I mean, what sort of choice is that? Eternal life really would be hell if you had to spend it with god. No, the church and the school thrive on power and authority. They need it. It's a handy replacement for reasoned logic and debate. Once you start questioning the system, the whole pack of cards just falls down. School Council elections are a joke, a waste of time and a distraction from the real issues affecting the studentry at Crookwell High. The only people who get elected are exactly those who don't question the system.

Greg shakes his head. "You're just being silly now. If you're so sure that the system can't be changed, why don't you try running yourself?"

"Come on Greg! Only nerdy turds get into the Council."

Greg is silent – a response which does little to foster our friendship. Well, all right then. I'll show him. I'll show all of them. Okay, damn it. I'll run for the Council. If I fail, then I am in the right. The system cannot be changed. But if I get in, well, I'll be a nerdy turd.

"And I can be your campaign manager!" says Greg excitedly.

Great! I've lost already!

Funnily enough, after a week of campaigning, the platform of Jennifer Dukes – my main opponent from Year Twelve – is that I shouldn't get on to the School Council exactly because I *am* a nerdy turd. Still, that's exactly what I expect from one of the Shirleys of 12C. I have always thought of her girlie clique as 'the Shirleys' because whenever you have the misfortune to look one in the eye, they return a facial expression of such ignorant condescension and pigheadedness that they could only be described as being, well, Shirleyish. Their lips curl in distaste, their brows furrow in irritation, and their eyeballs roll one hundred and eighty degrees. Needless to say, a lot of guys think that Jennifer and the Shirleys are quite attractive. I've spent many a lunchtime trying to figure out why. It has me stumped.

"...and I will always be there to listen to any problems you have and voice them to the Board. So vote for me. Thanks." Jennifer sits down to an appreciative round of applause and several prolonged wolf-whistles from the boys in the back row of the assembly hall. Richard quietens down after an angry stare from Kim. Deputy Kelly silences the remainder. There is no doubting that I am up against an empty-headed, populist, vote-crunching machine. And, equally, there is no doubting who will win. I move up to the lectern to speak.

My own speech is impassioned, but it shoots right over the heads of many of the students present, especially the jeering and cat-calling rough-head element. I try to explain the nature of power and authority that exists in the school structure. I extol as best I can the dubious benefits of having a student representative, before admitting that it doesn't make much difference either way in a totalitarian, religious, educational regime. I note Jennifer's claim that I am too nerdy for the Council and produce in defence a list of nerds that have made a fist of the position in the past. I criticise Jennifer's motivations in chasing the seat. I mean, does she really believe that future employers will give a damn whether she was on a school council elected by her peers? If she does, then *she* is the nerd – and a populist nerd at that. I promise that if the same peers vote for me, I will press for more student controls, subsidies on Monaco bars, and the abolition of god. Then I run out of time.

Of course, I'm expecting Jennifer to win in a landslide. I don't feel too bad about it. The whole exercise is just a thought experiment anyway. My failure to get elected will prove to me that I am not a nerdy turd (or, at the least, not as nerdy as Jennifer), and it will prove to Greg that the system cannot be changed. At least, I hope it does. Greg is of the opinion that I didn't give my best effort. But he is wrong there. I have given my all.

And, best of all, democracy will be the winner.

HAIR

"Gary, are you okay?"

It is Toni bending over my shoulder, concerned.

"Forget about the School Council elections, Gary. You'd have to be a real nerd to be elected for that." She glances about cautiously and whispers, "Jennifer's a bitch anyway. She thinks that she is *sooo* popular."

What? Does Toni think that I am upset over losing the crummy election? Hardly. To be quite honest, I haven't given a further moment's thought to it. But Toni seems to be quite naive about the political process. I must set her straight.

"Jennifer won the election because she *is* popular, Toni. That's how democracy works. The person who is most popular wins."

Why am I so unpopular?

Toni sits down beside me on the field and brushes a hand through her dark hair. "She's not popular with me. If it's any consolation, I voted for you."

No, this isn't much consolation. Obviously, Toni thinks that I am a real nerd. But she is off-beam in her assessment of my mental condition. I *like* to spend the odd lunchtime alone on the grass, depressed. It is one of the few pleasures I can afford myself at Crookwell High. Nothing makes me feel quite so good as spending an hour or so mulling over deep topics such as my unfortunate existence, the purposelessness of life in general, and my lack of confidence for the future. My soul sinks so low during these moments that, by the time the fifth period bell rings, I am almost deliriously happy to spend an hour in a classroom full of Shirleys, struggling with questions on monetary policy or free trade. I can't tell Toni this, however. Not that she is a Shirley by any means, but because she might come to the conclusion that I am suicidal and organise a meeting with the school chaplain, Old Ronny Wright. I have to lie.

"I don't care about the election, Toni... Ummm... I'm just allergic to something, that's all... It's been bugging me all day... Yeah, you know, it could even be the shampoo I used this morning." Hell. Can't I come up with something better than that?

Toni stares. "What sort of shampoo do you use?"

Jeez! "I don't know."

"Well you should know! Your hair is very fine. Using the wrong shampoo or conditioner could really damage it. No wonder it droops so much. Look at my hair. It's just as fine as yours, but I use a complete conditioning system with an amino concentrate which gives more bounce and body." She flicks her head from side to side while I duck for cover, shielding my eyes. "See?"

Indeed I can. I can see that I have managed to turn this conversation into a fashionable beauty commercial. Why is it that girls get so involved with their hair? Every day they come to school with curls, braids, ribbons, gel, mousse, and toolkits of brushes, combs, hairspray, bobbles and clips. They must take hours to get their hair organised for school each day. Thank god I'm a guy! We just let it sit on our heads like it should. No fussing about. Sure, my hair is getting a little long and curls about a bit, but this is more the result of good old-fashioned inactivity (I can't be bothered going to a hairdresser or barber or whatever) rather than the work of tedious organisation and planning. Hairs are just rods of dead cells anyway. They're nothing to get worked up about. In fact, I like girls with fairly short hair. They have a bit of spunk, a bit of bravado. But there aren't too many spunks at Crookwell High. Girls with short hair are accused of being feminists or dykes, effectively preventing them from being members of the Shirley clique, and the heaven-bound too, perhaps.

"Come with me to the Plaza after school today," says Toni. "I know this really good hairdresser. She'll turn you out a treat!"

I put my hands to my head protectively. "I'm happy the way my hair is, thank you. Really." I'm also a little angry. Why is Toni so eager for me to cut my hair? It doesn't look that bad, surely?

"Oh, come on, Gary. Mr Kelly will start hassling you soon about the length anyway," she replies knowingly.

I'm a little sceptical, but: "Yeah, okay."

The bell sounds for fifth period and we make our way over to our respective locker areas.

Toni has a point, I suppose. Kelly has already started making sly remarks about 'Rapunzel' and so forth. This is the first step in his plan. If I still turn up to school with long hair after a couple of weeks of being

Rapunzel, he will slip into stage two: physical harassment. Generally, he will issue a stream of demerits for petty crimes such as Being in Possession of Chewing Gum, Entering the School Grounds with the Shirt Hanging Out, or, my personal favourite, Not Having the Top Button Done Up Properly. Eventually, I will either get my hair cut or be expelled after collecting one thousand such demerits. It is not surprising, really, that a lot of guys from Crookwell High end up getting crew-cuts and mohawks. The school administration has absolutely no idea when it comes to student psychology.

"So, another mohawk?" asks the hairdresser, noticing the badge on my school blazer. I'm in the Plaza now. The hairdresser sees Toni sitting in the chair beside me. "Oh, hi there Toni."

"Hi Veronica. This is a friend of mine from school, Gary Kendall. He really needs a whole image makeover..."

"I'm fine, really."

"...I was thinking along the lines of a savage cut with black streaks to darken it up a bit. You know, more Gothic, kind of."

"My thoughts exactly, Toni. The dark look is really in right now." Veronica grabs a boxful of streaking gadgetry.

"Now just whoa there..."

"Stop fussing, Gary," scolds Toni. "The cap only hurts for a little while. Besides, you've got some nice length there. It would be a shame to let it go to waste. And streaking makes your hair less oily too! Less droopage."

Veronica stretches the streaking cap over my forehead and releases it with an audible 'Thwack!' Then she picks up a menacing metallic implement.

"Just watch where you stick that... *YOWW!*"

"Sorry. That's quite a knot you've got there, young man." Veronica continues to yank my fine filaments through several million microscopic holes in the streaking cap, an appliance which looks not entirely unlike an enlarged, coloured condom. I stare at my reflection in the mirror. Jesus Christ! My head looks like an advertisement for safe sex!

"Veronica knows how to deal with knotty hair," soothes Toni. "It's not going to hurt any more."

But the mirror reveals otherwise. I gasp in horror to see Sally McVey walk into the salon. She doesn't see me... perhaps if I pull this dryer down on my head... perhaps if I hide behind this large glossy edition of *Cleo*... perhaps she won't see me... perhaps...

"*Gary!* Is that you? Ha!"

Shit.

Sally is flabbergasted. She stares at Toni, then at me, and then back at Toni again. Toni purses her lips. Veronica drops her small jar of dye. The dryer suddenly releases a giant burst of steam and I gag on a mixture of water and streaking dye vapours.

"Oh my goodness! Ha ha ha *haaaaa...*" Sally collapses in a fit of laughter at the cashier, then races from the hairdressers with tears of mirth splashed across her face. I hear her echoes of hilarity bouncing around the Plaza for several minutes. It sounds like short bursts of machine-gun fire. Heck, it isn't that funny, surely? I start to panic. How am I going to hide the monstrosity on my melon from the school tomorrow? I will be a laughing stock! Still, no change there, I guess. But it is very worrying all the same.

Toni notices my troubled countenance and gives my hand a reassuring squeeze. "Don't worry Gary. You're going to turn out fine. The others from school just don't know fashion and style the way I do."

I suppress a small sigh.

That is exactly what I am worried about.

REALISM

Everyone I know thinks that I'm a pessimist, but I'm not really. True, I'm known to some of them as the Black Vortex of Despair, but they're exceptionally happy for human beings. Always partying, socialising, watching comedies and movies. For them, life is a seamless connection of *Happy Days* re-runs, popcorn and sleep. This is okay. *Happy Days* is funny enough (although terribly moralistic), popcorn's nice, and some of the best things happen in sleeping bags. But some things in life are pretty sad, too, and there are some horrible things that we can't avoid, like death and Christians.

I think I first stumbled across my more realist side (and it's *not* pessimism) during Bible class in Year Seven. It was sort of cosy and reassuring to think that the Earth and all the creatures on it were created by a really nice dude who floated about up in the sky, rewarding those who were good and slapping the wrists of those who swore or had their hands in their pockets during worship. But sometime during Years Seven and Eight the Bible story fell down rather badly. Are we saved by faith or works? Does humanity really have a choice to serve the skygod? Why did this really nice guy give Job a real shit of a weekend? Why say good stuff like "it's not nice to kill", then, in the words of the contemporary recorders, "smite" those who disagreed? Was Jesus, in this case, a PR expert thrown in for damage control? Did Jesus exist? Does proof of Jesus' existence somehow justify the belief in a skygod at all? Come to think of it, why did god put that stupid apple tree in the garden in the first place if she knew that the outcome was going to be a heck of a lot of pain, sorrow, war and death – all in her glory?

What a dork.

Greg shakes his head beside me. "What did you do to your hair, Gary?"

"Forget the hair, Greg. I'm talking about god."

"Oh well, you know what I think. It's beyond the power of mortal men..."

"And women."

"...*and* women to try to understand the Mind of God." He returns to copying my answers to the Maths assignment on to a blank piece of paper.

It is lunchtime. We are seated on the edge of the school field: Greg writing, me thinking, and several good-looking Year Nine girls playing hockey. I think: but if Adam and Eve (according to the tale) were immortal at first, then, by Greg's reasoning, they *both* should have understood the 'Mind of God' before all the sinning started! Eve was thus knowledgeable, but stupid, or at least a little unconcerned about what her actions would do to countless generations. Adam was no better, but he was excusable from blame as his action was more the response of a lover who could not bear to live forever without his girl. Sick, but sort of romantic. Anyway, the damage was done. And though some contemporary feminist writers have described Eve's actions as a rallying cry for women against patriarchal authority figures, I can only hope the current crop have more success.

But Greg disagrees vehemently with my thesis, and argues that God is a Good Bloke who gave humanity the freedom to choose between Him and an apple, and the fact that Eve happened to prefer Golden Delicious to Eternal Life is just our bad luck, or words to that effect.

"And I wouldn't be surprised if God struck you down with a bolt of lightning for thinking such a terrible thing against Him," he adds fiercely.

This is meant to shock me (no pun intended) into accepting his point of view. Of course, Greg is awfully afraid of death. I think that it is this fear which keeps him on the straight and narrow path which leads to heaven's pearly gates. I'm a little unsure myself. No one has been known to survive death (okay, okay, I hear the Christians shouting about Lazurus and Jesus, but, even accepting this tale, two people out of the ten billion or so who have ever lived is a lousy success rate), and so it is bound to be an unsettling experience, one that I hope I will experience only after I have experienced everything else I want to experience, if you catch my drift. But it is certainly something that, one day, I'll *want* to experience. Not now. Now I'm young and awfully vibrant. But some day I won't be. Some day I'll want out. I'm sort of glad the escape hatch is there. I don't crave the eternal life offered by the skygod. I'm sure that path would eventually lead to insanity.

Greg finishes copying my answers. We sit together and watch the Year Nine girls play hockey until the bell for fifth period rings. Then, as we pack up, a terrible thought strikes me.

"Greg...?"

"Yeah?"

"If we all lived forever in heaven, would my grandmother appear to me as my grandmother? You know, all old like? Or would she look younger, like... ahh... Toni for instance?" This sort of thing has troubled me for a while now. Religion seems to be full of unsolvable conundrums, problems and inconsistencies.

But Greg just stares.

"You're really sick, Gary."

II
LIFE SENTENCES

HELP

Being one of the only atheists in a religious school is interesting at times. Morning roll call and worship with Ms French is always a lot of laughs – as is Bible – but a heap of fun also occurs in the precious moments before a vital assessment or exam. It's amazing just how many heads are lifted to the heavens in prayer – a silent 'help!' to the Great Quiz Mistress in the sky.

"Before we start the test, let us offer a prayer to Jesus," says Mrs Lowe before another Maths assessment.

I can see Greg, out of the corner of my eye, bowing his head and closing his eyes in all earnestness. So does just about everyone else in the room, giving me the chance to take one last swig from my brandy flask which I keep hidden inside my blazer. I'd be dead if I were caught with it in the school grounds. Fortunately, no one sees the manoeuvre. They're all too busy talking with god. I wonder what they think she'll do for them. God can't give everyone an 'A'. The dubious scaling procedures take care of that. Still, they seem to take enough comfort in the prayer. Perhaps that's all they've got. I wish I could relax like they could, without having to resort to the brandy flask.

I didn't always drink heavily before exams. I used to be really cool and relaxed about the whole assessment thing. But now, in Year Twelve, I'm always nervous before an assessment task, especially those which have a direct bearing on my HSC, and thus the rest of my life. Oh, I study diligently enough of course. But no matter how much effort you put in beforehand, it all comes down to how you feel on the day. Jacko, Sandhurst's aging star half, knows what I mean, judging from what he says in his autobiography, *Jacko!*. He reckons that you can train long and hard during the week before the title decider, but if you're not one hundred percent at the kick-off, you'll be hard up to be lifting the cup at full-time. (I know that his coach once said something akin to 'winning starts on Monday', but it also finishes on the Saturday or Sunday, and it's about time someone made this obvious point instead of accepting dumb sporting allegories at face value.)

Let's get one thing straight though. I'm not an alcoholic or anything. I just need to slow my mind down a little, that's all. It gets terribly overactive before an exam. That's what my stress psychologist, Dr Newth, told me when I saw him in the holiday break before the start of Year Eleven. Mum thought it might be useful for me to see one of these quacks about my nervous dry-retching after reading an article on the HSC in the newspaper.

"Sit down, Gavin," Dr Newth had intoned. His speech was slow and soporific – no doubt meant to be soothing – but it sounded to me as though he had swallowed an entire packet of Prozac and other assorted valium products.

"It's Gary actually."

"Gary?" The man doddered and cocked his head. "Ahh, Gary. Yes. I'm sorry. Gavin was a former HSC student I advised who... ahhh, well. Hmmm. Very unfortunate. Hmmm. Shocking." He shook his head wistfully.

"Dr Newth?"

"Hmmm? Yes, Gary?"

"Can we start?"

He slowly nodded his head. "Yes, hmmm. Let's, ahhh, begin."

So I had explained to Dr Newth as best I could the problems I was having coping with HSC stress: my inability to eat anything before simple tests, my nauseous dry-retching before (and sometimes during) in-class essays and assignments, my fear of failure, the failure itself and, most of all, the fear of the fear. Indeed, most of the time I feared the actual stress-sickness, instead of the exam. It was just awful! I knew that I had large reservoirs of potential, somewhere, deep inside me, but I was so afraid of being stressed out that I managed to worry myself to the point of incapacitation anyway. Any study I did, I argued to Dr Newth, would be wasted because, on the day, I would not be able to face going into that dreaded examination room. I mean, this was the HSC! This was the most important test that any kid had to face. Stuff it up, and the chances of getting into a good uni course were pretty well nullified. Without a degree, I would never forge a career, make lots of money, attract girls and... and, well, do anything really. My life would be consigned to scraping the fat off the grills at McDonalds, selling ice-creams at the cricket, or becoming a chartered accountant. The pressure was on to succeed, and I knew that I needed help.

After an eternity of nodding and pondering, Dr Newth devised a strategy to combat my HSC nerves. It was the tried and true Four Point Plan: (a) I had to live one day at a time, (b) I had to find time in my pressing schedule to relax and meditate to several soundtracks of Dr Newth's voice, (c) I had to organise my time effectively, and (d) I had to think *positive*.

"Ahhh, your anxiety Gav- errr Gary," the good doctor had elucidated, "is just an indication that your mind is ready to go. You cram your head full of knowledge and it wants to be unleashed. Ahhh, yes, that's it. Just imagine the anxiety as being the dog, straining on the leash. Hmmm."

"A *dog?*"

"Hmmm? Yes. A dog. The stress is just your mind telling you that it is full of information, ready to go. It is a perfectly natural reaction, but it can be taken too far. Yes, whenever you feel that you are becoming too stressed, just remember your relaxation exercises and your breathing. Ahhh Gavin, remember that the HSC is not everything in life. Remember to live one day at a time, hmmm?"

And I did live one day at a time too! For weeks in Year Eleven, I was cool and calm while the first HSC assessment loomed in my diary. I pushed it out of my mind – it was not on *today*, and I lived for *today*. I listened to Dr Newth's soothing voice on my tape-recorder and became at peace with my inner being. I studied as he told me I should – accumulating knowledge teaspoon by teaspoon, instead of gulping whole textbooks down my throat the night before. I practiced my breathing. And on the day of that first assessment – a Biology test – I was fully prepared. I could feel the dog straining on the leash. My teaspoons of knowledge were ready to go!

"Hey Gary!" Kim had exclaimed outside the door to the Biology room. "Study hard? This test looks like a real horror."

The dog pulled a little harder.

"I think I did enough." I closed my eyes and took a deep breath.

Kim returned to her notes. "You know this test is worth twenty percent of the Biology assessments?"

"Yeah."

"Funny, you know. With fifty percent of the HSC taken up by assessments now, that makes this test worth ten percent of the final Biology grade. To think that we can have so much weight placed on our performance in Year Eleven! I thought it was Year Twelve that counted!"

I took another breath. The leash was tightening in my hand.

"And considering that the two units of Biology make up, for me at any rate, one-sixth of my total marks, that makes the test worth, uhh, one point six six recurring percent of the final HSC score."

The dog had mutated from a poodle to a doberman. I wrapped the leash around its nose. My stomach rumbled and turned. "Just shut up about it, okay Kim?"

"Sure." She glanced at her notes once more.

I tried to push the nerves from my mind.

"You're not nervous are you? Just because this test can mean the difference between you getting one hundred or ninety-eight point three three recurring percent? Don't worry about it. Worrying about it only makes it worse."

The dog chewed through the leash and sprinted off out of control, my teaspoons of knowledge flying along in its wake.

"Hey Gary! Where are you going? The test starts in five minutes!"

But I was already around the corner and racing for the toilets. I was never good with animals. And as I retched into the bowl, I could only take solace in the fact that I *had* managed to live one day at a time.

It was just my luck that that day – exam day – turned out to be a real bastard.

DUPLICITY

I hate the days when teachers hand back tests or exams, especially those tests where one has spent the first fifteen minutes dry-retching into a toilet bowl. There is an air of excitement, suspense, and for some like me, an overwhelming sense of dread. I know what is coming. Although most of my friends call me a pessimistic worry-wart, I'm usually very accurate in predicting my mark. I pride myself in this. My feelings are honest. Of course, it would be nice to think that one did very well, but somehow I always know when I've done less than good.

"Kendall!"

"Here." I walk the long metres to Ms French's desk, take the paper, and return to my seat. Only then do I check the mark. Yep. Another fifty-eight. It is my modal score for English this year. Every test I do, every essay I write, seems to bring me back a fifty-eight. This cannot be mere coincidence. Perhaps Ms Amy French just sees my name on the top of the page and writes 'fifty-eight' in red ink to save time. Well next time I won't bother sitting her tests at all. I'll just write my name on a piece of paper, hand it in to the lazy cow, and toddle off to the library to finish my other assessments. That'll save *me* some time.

"How did you go?" whispers Greg, his eyes conspiratorial.

"Stuffed. Fifty-eight again."

"Oh, it's not that bad..."

Jeez! Greg really annoys me sometimes. His voice is consoling and sympathetic, but I know he is slightly relieved. And he should know that I know, if he has any grip at all on HSC psychology. He knows the ranking system, how it works. Everyone in the class is given a rank according to how well they perform on their assessments. This rank is then used in calculating the final HSC score. My bombing out just gives people like Greg some additional breathing space. The knife-edged competitiveness of the HSC brings out the worst in everyone. We all want to succeed. We all want to get a good rank. But that means that we are all mentally willing the others to stuff up. Every screwed-up test by someone else boosts our own chances of survival. However, if we want to remain on cuddly terms with everyone, it is important that we bottle these awkward feelings inside. We have to be two-faced. We have to say things like 'sorry mate' or 'bad luck' when all the time we are thinking 'thank god' – if we are unsure about our own position – or 'sucked in badly!' – if we just like being vindictive bastards. Yeah, good old competition. It is so pleasing to see it in education.

But I'm fed up with being on cuddly terms with Greg.

"Spin on this." I raise my index finger surreptitiously behind my back, away from the probing eye of Ms French, who returns the friendly smile which I have spread-eagled across my dial. If I'm going down, I might as well take a few good souls with me. It feels good too. Yes, I think I like being honest.

Duplicity surrounds me in this school. I see it now in Greg, and in the intense faces of the others in the class as they await the test results. I see it in the cretinous Deputy Kelly, who tries hard to get along with the students he isn't busting for hairstyle offences, but who no doubt betrays us all in torrid Board meetings or on parent-teacher nights. And, horribly, I saw its hideous face last lunchtime in the terrible events which took place in Old Ronny's Bible room.

It had happened fairly quickly. Richard and I had been playing a game of table-tennis – it's the only game we know where our skills are roughly similar. During a particularly long, plonking rally, Jennifer Dukes and some of her clique cronies wandered up behind Richard. She greeted me with one of her typical Shirley looks which caused me to mistime a slicing backhand half-volley. The ball disappeared underneath a desk on the other side of the room. I went over to fetch it. Bending under a chair, I found myself eye-to-eye with Kim, whom I knew to be Richard's better half. She yanked me down under the table with her, putting a finger against her lips. *Be quiet. Don't give me away.* Surprised, I did so. I thought: *what the hell is she up to?* It didn't take me too long to figure it out. Queen Jennifer was sitting on the table-tennis table, her legs spread just a little, smiling at Richard. It occurred to me that I was observing an elaborate case of entrapment, with Richard as the victim. I could hear the words exchanged.

"Do you like me, Richard?"

"In some ways."

"People hate me you know. They think I'm snobby."

I could not believe it. Jennifer really sounded upset!

"Well sometimes..."

"It's really hard to get by when no one likes you. Do you know what it's like?"

"Not everyone thinks you're a... a..."

"A bitch, right?" She laughed wryly. "You can say it, Richard. People hate me at this school."

"I wouldn't say I *hate* you..."

"But you'd never go with me, right?"

"I didn't say that."

"So you would think about it then? Are you going with anyone right now?"

"Well, sorta..."

"You wouldn't even go with me for a little while? Just a week or so? Am I as bad as that?" She leaned back on the table and sighed.

I wanted to warn Richard of the danger, but Kim held her hand across my mouth. Surely Richard would wonder where I had got to with the table-tennis ball? Wasn't he a little suspicious? Couldn't he see how stupid, how utterly *ridiculous,* the whole scene was?

"Yeah. Sure. What the hell."

No. I guess not.

At that moment, Kim leaped up from underneath the desk. She paused before the door to the Bible room – just long enough for Richard to see how upset she was – then fled out into the playground. Jennifer slid off the table and lowered her skirt back down to a more moral level.

"You're a bastard, Richard. We warned Kim that you were. She wouldn't believe us until now."

Then she and her cronies had left, silent as death, righteously proud that they had brought another poor sinner to judgement. At first Richard just stood by the table, stunned, his right hand clutching the green table-tennis paddle. I emerged, rather feebly, from underneath the desk, holding up the ball triumphantly. Somehow, I don't think he thought that I had spent the last five minutes looking for it. Then he sat down in a chair and sighed.

I've seen this 'entrapment' scenario before. It was on one of those dumb American talk shows on the telly during one of my sickies. These women came on the show and told a studio of complete strangers how they had set up their husbands to test their fidelity. One had hired a model to flirt with her husband. Another had hired a private detective to follow her husband on business trips. A third had locked herself in her bedroom wardrobe for three days to see if her man brought anyone else home. She was supposed to have been on a holiday in Quebec. And, following in the traditions of these trashy shows, Kim had organised

Jennifer Dukes to offer herself unto Richard as a test of his loyalty.

Right now, in Ms French's English class, I can only think about how insecure these people are, how duplicitous, and how ignorant of the male psyche. Did they really think that their guys would stoutly resist the temptation thrust before them? If they did, they should get their heads out of naive romance novels. Guys will take a bit of sexual pleasure anywhere they can, from anybody. Take it from me. It doesn't mean that they necessarily like the person involved. It's just a normal male reaction to the situation. Sex offered. Sex taken. No big deal. No love involved. Believe me, setting up your partner only leads to disaster.

Anyway, does Kim really feel betrayed in this? Does she really think that Richard could possibly like Jennifer? Toni knows she's just a bitch. We all do.

But what hurts me the most is that we were all guilty of deception. Jennifer deceived Richard into thinking she liked him. Richard went along with the subterfuge, knowing (I hope) that he held no real feelings for Jennifer. I stayed silent at the crucial moment, when a good friend would have warned him of the danger. And Kim, probably worried that Richard didn't like her any more, set the whole thing up. It ended up hurting all of us, except for Jennifer. Now I wonder if she was more involved? As Iago said in *Othello*: "Knavery's plain face is never seen till used." But what do I know? Who am I kidding with this hokey analysis?

I only got fifty-eight for my Shakespeare essay.

OPTOMETRISTS

School yearbooks are terrible things. By accessing the correct shelf in the school library, any Crookwell High student can see first-hand how nerdy one seemed in Years Seven and Eight, that savage haircut in Year Nine, the boggling glasses in Year Ten, the 'closed-eyes' look in Year Eleven... Heck! School photos are a menace, and their annual publication in the school mag, *Kaleidoscope,* should be banned outright. It is no wonder that I get absolutely nowhere with any of the girls in the school. With my looks in Years Seven and Eight, I really was facing an uphill struggle. Meanwhile, newcomers like Richard have a past that is not so easily traced. I think a lot of girls would baulk at the sight of his Year Seven photo. Everyone is ugly in Year Seven. Well, everyone at Crookwell High is at any rate. Linda Travers, for one, has definitely improved since. So has Toni. And Sally? Well, judging between her Year Seven and Year Eleven photos, I'm fairly undecided. If anything, I think she may have gone downhill.

In fact, after some of the things which have gone on this year, such as the Peter Woolley Scandal and the Great Hairdo Incident, I'm not even sure if I like her any more. I don't think I like anyone. And I'm starting to feel comfortable about it too.

"I thought I'd find you here." Toni sits down next to me on our designated position by the edge of the field. "Where is everyone today?"

I shrug my shoulders. "Greg's up in the library writing an English essay." The HSC assessments are now on in earnest. I managed to finish my little number on Emily Dickinson earlier this morning. Her poetry is cram-packed with images of sexual repression. And I should know – sexual repression is my forte. "Richard's trying out with the basketball team, I think. Where's Kim?"

"She didn't turn up today. She's probably sick, but... Gary, I just heard Jennifer talking at the tuckshop. Have you heard about anything happening between Richard and Kim?"

I hate to lie, but: "No..."

"Oh, she's probably just sick then." She looks at my reading materials and squeals. "Oh God! *Kaleidoscope!* Oh Gary, don't look at it. I look like a complete nut." She confiscates the publications and starts perusing the Year Seven edition. "Oh my God! My hair is a disaster. I know it was fashionable then, but hey! Times sure change."

"We all look like nuts," I note sympathetically. "Just check out those windscreens I was wearing back then. They made my eyes look like golf balls."

"Where are you?" Toni flicks through some pages. "Ahh, there. Hmmm. Oh they're not that bad, Gary."

"Give me a break! I should have been the monster in *The Fly!*"

"No way." Toni grins cheekily. "Though you would have made a perfect Toad in *Toad of Toad Hall.*"

"Yeah, thanks a lot." I pretend to be upset and swing my fist against her shoulder. She falls on her back and groans melodramatically.

"Oh get up..."

"Okay." She raises herself up on her elbows and rubs some grass from her blue school jumper. Then she picks out some more damning *Kaleidoscopes.* "You changed your frames in Year Ten, but I think I prefer the ones you have now. Oh wow. Look at me! Gel was really in during Year Ten, wasn't it. Ughh." She looks up, her face brightening. "You haven't thought of getting contacts by any chance?"

Contacts? Of *course* I have thought about getting contacts. Contacts are the dream of all unfortunate sods like myself who are forced to wear glasses. Glasses are simply ancient – they were invented in the Middle Ages! So much for the so-called 'technological age' in which I find myself. Glasses transform likeable people such as myself into walking nightmares. I hate them. I've always hated them. Stupid, wiry, metallic contraptions with hoops of molten sand that are always dirty, fall out during tennis, and make your eyes either look like pin-pricks or watermelons depending on your prescription. And they are an undoubted hindrance when it comes to attracting women. How many advertisements do you see where the heroic male figure has four eyes? Even in commercials for glasses, the man is always seen *taking them off* whilst the woman keeps hers on. It's outright discrimination. Lois Lane only found her Superman when Mr Kent removed his peepers in a phone-booth. He took off a lot of other stuff as well, I guess, but I think it was fairly important to remove his horn-rims before flying off to save the world. All the 'beast-to-beauty' stories on the telly have one common theme: the beasts wear glasses, braces, have daggy hair and drive Volkswagons, while the beauties are frame-free, possess brilliant white teeth, stylish hair, and drive Volkswagons. The link is similarly noted by advertising gurus and mechanics.

Earlier this year, whilst yet again retrieving a displaced lens from the toilet bowl, I decided that enough was enough. I was going to the optometrists for a pair of contacts and nothing was going to stand in my way, especially not the coffee table which I had tripped over on the way out.

Optometrists, on the whole, are rather friendly. They're not in the same league as dentists. They don't waggle their fingers at you when your eyesight deteriorates. They don't say "Oh my God! I've never seen someone with such poor..." or "Why haven't you seen me over the past ten years?" They just sit there and shine a bright torch in your face.

"Oh my God!" my optometrist, Dean, had said as he peered into the aqueous humor of my left eyeball. "What the hell have we got here?"

I shuffled my feet nervously. "Uh, what exactly?"

"My God...!"

"Yeah, yeah..."

Dean put the torch down and gripped my hand. "I just want you to know there is nothing abnormal about your condition."

"What condition?" I started to panic.

"Oh nothing. There was nothing you could have done."

"What are you talking about? I feel as though I'm at the dentist's."

After much fussing, Dean had eventually informed me that I could never wear contacts as I had "unnaturally-shaped eyeballs". I had never heard of such a condition, but I believed it after trying to place the little transparent bastards on them. Heck, it was a disaster. I've always had a fear of sticking things in or on my eyes. It's a natural, defensive reaction. Really, the things that some people do to make themselves more attractive nowadays! Forget about liposuction or facelifts. These procedures can be performed while the patient is unconscious anyway. Nothing compares to holding an eyelid open with one hand whilst the other tries to force a small, plastic pellet on to your frankly startled iris.

And it was only my tears of frustration which managed to get them out again.

Dean had observed my anguish with more than due sympathy. "Come on, Gary. We'll get you some new frames. You won't recognise yourself. They're nice. Really." He patted me consolingly on the shoulder.

In this intimate moment of male bonding, I decided to tell Dean my *real* reason for getting contacts. He listened thoughtfully and nodded his head. "It's natural to feel that way, but I don't think you're right. Some women tell me that glasses make a man seem more intelligent, compassionate, more desirable. For others, the fact of whether you wear glasses or not doesn't even cross their minds. When they see you, they don't see your hulking frames at all. They just see you."

I started to feel a little better then. What dentist would give you thoughtful advice like that? None. They are all too worried about money, bridgework, extraction, and why you haven't brushed your teeth after every meal for the last ten years. I thought that Dean was a really understanding bloke. After a while, it struck me that Dean never wore glasses himself, nor did any of the other optometrists in the practice. I thought it strange that all the optometrists I knew had twenty-twenty vision.

"Are you kidding?" Dean had grinned. "We all have trouble with our eyes. But I wear contacts. If I had to wear glasses, I'd look a right dork."

So there it was. I was condemned to look like a dork for all eternity, or until medical science shifted its arse into gear to help people like myself. That realisation was a mortal blow, one of the saddest moments in my life.

But Toni is laughing. She thinks it is just about the funniest thing she has ever heard.

That's life for you, I suppose.

NOTHING

What happens when we die?

Heck, I know I'm not the first to ask that question. Nor will I be the last. But I've been a practicing philosopher for several years now, so I think that my view should count for something.

My grandfather, on Dad's side, died when I was in Year Seven. Dad explained that he had Alzheimer's disease, but I had thought at the time that he said "Old Timer's" and so it became set in my head that all old people died that way; that old age itself became a disease that only death could cure. In my grandfather's case, Old Timer's disease meant that he kept forgetting things. It was little things at first, like where he had put his coffee or who had won the Cup in '77. Then, almost overnight, gaping holes appeared in his memory. He thought he was back in London during the Blitz, and I guess living next to Sandhurst railway station didn't help. Once he was convinced that he had seen his long-dead sister in a nearby shopping mall. He stubbornly resisted the notion that he was married, preferring to think of his wife as a friend who slept over occasionally. After a while he couldn't recognise me, Sarah, Mum, or even Dad – his only child. He would wake up early some mornings and set forth on great adventures. On more than one occasion, Dad and I had to scour the streets looking for him. We usually found him on the Great Western Highway, marching proudly towards Rundle, trying to open up a second front against Hitler. Eventually, the only thing he could remember was his army identification number, though he would rarely let us know what it was, for fear that we were 'the enemy'. Then he forgot that.

And there was nothing left.

I remember that I couldn't bring myself to cry at his funeral. I looked with envy at Sarah and Mum, whose faces were torn with anguish. Even Dad cried. He had lost his own father. For the first time in my life I looked deep inside myself. Why can't I cry? What happens when we die?

Nobody seems to consider this question much at school. We are all too stuffed with life: Toni and Kim are engrossed in *Cleo,* Sally is preoccupied with developing a reverse swing delivery, and Richard prefers to talk about girls and the weekend footy. Greg is the only person I know who has even mentioned death – and he thinks that it is only a temporary stop-over point before we get shuttled off to heaven or hell. This lack of interest is unwarranted. Death is the great equaliser. It's something we must all face eventually. No matter what our successes or failures, our riches and fame or lack thereof, we are united by the fact that we will surely die some day. Whatever we have done, whoever we are, we shall all crumble to dust.

So, in line with my egalitarian nature, I thought that I should find out as much as I could about this death thing before I had to face it myself. I spent my lunchtimes in Year Seven reading books in the school library.

I came across several theories about death. (As no one has been on the other side, and returned, I could not find any factual evidence.) Greg's view is that of your typical Christian moral crusader: death is just one step away from judgement. When you die, you stand in this big room where god holds the book of life. She opens the book and traces all the good and bad things you've done. If she thinks you're good enough, you get to live again for eternity with god and Greg. Otherwise, you live again for eternity in hell, where demons prod you with rods of hot iron and force you to watch endless re-runs of *The Partridge Family.* This line is similar to other Christian religions, except that in more liberal churches the idea of hell is dropped to make way for a more compassionate god figure, though, of course, heaven stays. Another major difference is that Greg believes that god will traipse down to Earth to judge some of the living as well. Apparently, too many people have been asking god for redemption on their deathbeds, making a mockery of the whole judgemental process. The threat that judgement could come at any time keeps people on their toes.

I also read of other religions which promote the idea that we have eternal souls that are 're-born' when our physical being dies – though what we come back as seems open to debate. Firm moral principles dictate that the 'bad' come back as something worse than what they were – like slugs or snails or politicians. Sometimes the crime can determine what you come back as – Nazis come back as Jews, communists come back as small-l liberals, libertarians come back as dictators and so on. Meanwhile, the 'good' have greater health and riches bestowed upon them in future reincarnations. If this theory is true, then the super-rich owner of the new city casino, Kurt Powell, must be Mahatma Ghandi one generation on. Perhaps that is why so many people treat the rich with deep respect. It's curious that both Christian and non-Christian beliefs tend to link wealth with moral purity.

However, the reality is likely to be less interesting than the theory. I've got this gut feeling that I'm only going to get one chance. When I die, I won't be tormented in hell or paraded into heaven. I just won't be. Nothing. Absolute unbeing. Non-existence. It's like my grandfather's funeral. The dead thing in the coffin was no longer my grandfather. It was just a mass of chemical materials. He had died long before, even before his heart had stopped beating. He had died when he ceased to remember who he was. Old Timer's disease had taken him from us. I was sad, of course. But I think I was more sorry for myself, or Sarah, or Dad. We would never see him again. And for all of humankind's perceived greatness, we still cannot prevent people from dying.

Most disturbing to the ego is that nothing changes when we die. There is no natural salute or tribute to our passing: the moon continues to orbit the Earth, the Earth still moves around the sun, our solar system will keep existing on the edge of a galactic spiral arm, whole galaxies will continue to shift in the vast seas of space, the stars will still shine upon the Earth and the Earth will still rotate upon its axis to give us day and night. That is, until about four billion years from now when the sun burns up all its fuel and explodes.

Tell someone that they will die within a century and they shrug their shoulders. But tell the same person that four billion years from now the sun will self-destruct, destroying all life in the solar system, and you may get a more serious reaction.

As if it matters.

GRADES

Life is nothing but a long series of judgements. Every day we are assessed by others according to the clothes we wear, the jobs we take, the money we make, the friends we have, the car we drive, the train we catch, the station we catch the train from, the place we live, the colour of our skin, the people we vote for, the music we listen to, the religious beliefs we hold, the beliefs we scorn, the football teams we support, the football teams we don't, the football teams we really couldn't give a damn about one way or the other but as both reach the final a subconscious choice has to be made, the type of movies we go and see, the places we like to go to relax, the shows we most enjoy on television, the views we hold on Indonesia's invasion of East Timor, the world figures we admire, the world figures we would rather see dead, the local figures we would rather see dead, the number of times we get out and party, the parties we are seen attending, and the number of times we actually got out and partied and woke up the next morning wishing we were dead.

Everything we do, every move we make is analysed, judged and given a grade by someone: parents, brothers, sisters, friends, that girl at the party you threw up over but can't remember her name, god (if you're religious), yourself (if you're not), peers, teachers, just about everyone really. Every time you walk out the door, you are facing another societal test or examination.

It would drive you crazy if you thought about it all the time, but, luckily enough, we have been schooled to ignore it. Because from the ages of four or five to sixteen or seventeen – from kindergarten to Year Twelve – we are constantly reminded about how others perceive us through the comments on our school grade reports. I make a pretty good fist of ignoring these ridiculous half-yearly personality caricatures whenever they show up. How can anyone take them seriously? Especially parents. They've been through school. They above all should know that teachers don't know the first thing about you, so why they take an unnecessary interest in the 'comments' section is beyond me.

"Gary, your mother and I have been reading some of the comments in your school report and, well, we decided it was time for a little chat." Dad sits down in his favourite chair, the dreaded school report on his lap. Mum has her arms folded against her chest. Dad points me towards the spare seat.

I'm prepared for the worst. Apprehension swells up within me. I lean into the chair and grip its arm-rests in anticipation.

"Let's start with English."

Heck. My English teacher, Ms French, isn't on my Christmas card list, that's for sure. She never understands the brilliance of my double entendres or the clever innuendos in my creative writing pieces. And she positively disregards my thesis that the poetry of Emily Dickinson is riddled with sexual allusion and metaphor. I suppose it is because she is just as repressed as that American poet. She is a typical, moralistic, wowser Christian. She never wants to see the sexual side of anything. No wonder that *Puberty Blues* isn't on Crookwell High's reading list for the HSC! I would've liked to have seen her squirm her way through that without discussing sex. Instead, the class has to yawn its way through bloody *Lord Jim.*

Dad nods approvingly as he reads: "Gary has worked very hard all this semester. A tremendous effort."

Oh hell! This is even worse than I had expected. And the comments from all my other subjects are roughly similar. It is simply awful. Maths: "Gary has achieved a pleasing standard". Biology: "Gary is improving all the time". Bible: "Gary has demonstrated an enthusiastic and solid grasp of the subject". Physics: "It's good to see that Gary has achieved what he aimed for". Economics: "Very consistent"; and Modern History: "An excellent effort". This is terrible, and the only consolation I can take from this willy-nilly string of pseudo-analysis is that a couple of the comments, especially those from Physics and Eco, are sufficiently ambiguous to be taken either way. In nearly every comment I am painted as being 'conscientious' (of all things), and, reading what it means from my ever-present pocket dictionary, I am terribly upset. Conscientious! I am nothing of the sort. I am the exact opposite. I am an intellectual who rebels against the Establishment as represented by the likes of the teachers and their creed. Can't they see that? Can't they see who I really am? Heck, even in Year Eight I was an agitator, a dissident. Everything I made in metalwork turned out to be a bottle-opener. Couldn't they see the tragic symbolism even then? I don't deserve this.

"However, while you probably feel happy with these comments," continues my father in a graver tone, "they do not quite accord with your marks."

Oh no.

I listen, horrified, as Dad blurts forward a series of numbers which, while not being disproportionately low (compared to other years), are nonetheless not going to qualify me for Dux or the coveted Egerton-Warburton prize for excellence.

"Fifty-four, sixty-seven, fifty... What does the 'p' next to the fifty mean, Gary?"

"Pass, I think." Or perhaps provisional. Who cares? It's Bible. Atheists are supposed to fail Bible. God knows how I got fifty.

"...fifty-eight, sixty-one, sixty-one and sixty-nine." Dad folds the report and places it back on his lap. I know what is coming. "Gary, we're both very proud of you putting in an effort and all that. But what your mother and I would like to know is, if you were putting in such a good effort, then how could your marks be so atrocious?" He shakes his head in incomprehension.

Oh hell. This is the very worst kind of report. 'Conscientious' remarks are bad enough, but to be classified as a *try-hard* is the very lowest of the low. Dad mentions something about seeking professional help – tutors and the like – but I'm not really listening. The teachers don't really know who I am or what I can become. They don't know my real talents. How can they? All they see at school is a short, scruffy character, who is always late to class, eats Monaco bars from the canteen, and watches the Year Nine girls play hockey on the field during Modern History. I hardly breathe a word to anybody except to my closest friends. Teachers take my alternative stance on the subjective as a sign of 'missing the point', being unnecessarily argumentative, or just plain wrong. Heck, there's no absolute right or wrong anyway. I'm right about that. I'm just different, that's all. I'm a free spirit. I have a mind which is unique and, unlike Greg and many others, relatively untouched by the religious twaddle pervading the curriculum. And some day I'll prove them wrong about me. One day they will all witness the dangerous rebel that lurks deep within; the rebel that is ready to risk all and lash out against an unjust Society in all its forms, no matter what the personal cost.

But first I've got to finish the HSC and get into a good uni.

WHEELS

Mankind became truly civilised after the invention of the wheel, or so it said in my Year Ten Ancient History notes. The wheel – an ingenious, circular device – enabled the easier and speedier transportation of rock, lumber and the other raw materials necessary to build shelters, fight wars and develop the frisbee.

Five thousand years later, the wheel is used by my peers to impress girls.

I am sitting outside the local Motor Registry, depressed. The last two weeks have been a real nightmare, and the troubles all started when Richard turned up at my house in his new car.

"Hey, Gary, check it out my man!" he coaxed from his position in the sheepskin-covered driving seat. "Dad said he'd let me have it when I passed my driving test."

I had quickly glanced over the machine that was parked in our driveway, all a-gleam in the mid-morning sun. To be quite honest, I don't know the first thing about cars. All I know is that they have a body (a 'chassis' or something), an engine somewhere underneath the bonnet or boot, and four wheels. But I did my best to look impressed.

"Hey! A Torana!" I exclaimed after noting the metal label on the back. "Green too. Wow. And what a chassis! Not a dent. Engine sounds great. Nice wheels. The back tyres are rather large..."

"Mag wheels, my man. Twin exhaust, tinted windows..."

"It's a nice shade of green."

"Uh, yeah, I suppose." Richard switched the engine off. "Look Gary, I'm going to drive her into school tomorrow. See how she runs."

"But what about the train and bus?" I demanded. This was disastrous. Richard was the only guy I could talk to on the morning train trip from Sandhurst railway station. Because Greg comes in from the Rundle line, I don't see him until the bus trip to school from Crookwell station. That's all the company I have. All of the other students have their own cliques and gangs to talk to. They get very rowdy at times, and take scant regard of my white shirt which signifies my status as a school senior.

Richard smiled. "Forget the train, man. Forget the bus. I'll pick you up in the Frog." He patted the door of the 'Frog' affectionately. "Besides, I need to get Kim back. Hopefully she'll go wild over it. I'll ask her whether she'd like to be driven home. It will give me a chance to explain what a total mess I've made of things, and find out whether she wants me back."

I screwed up my face. "You're going to ask her for *forgiveness*?"

"No, no man. Well. Yeah. Kinda. Just don't tell anyone okay? I've got a reputation to maintain. I know you can keep a secret. If Kim still hates me, then, well I could always start a rumour with Greg about how I dumped her first." He settled into the driver's seat and gripped the steering wheel. "Hopefully, it won't come to that. Hopefully, I'll be making a few 'detours' on the way home..." He flashed me the most unsubtle wink I had ever seen.

Yeah. Right. I jumped out of the car. Richard promised to pick me up for school the following day before driving off. I watched him negotiate the corner at the bottom of my street, then moved back inside the house. Thoughts of wheels and girls troubled me as I tackled my Physics homework on circular motion that evening. Eventually I fell asleep.

But Richard was right about the connection between wheels and girls. As soon as the Frog pulled into the schoolyard on Monday morning, we were swamped by the attentions of some rather attractive Year Ten sorts. Even Sally and Linda were impressed by Richard's set of wheels. I remained cool and composed in the front seat while Richard showed them the gears, crankshafts and other gizmos under the hood. The whole school seemed a-buzz about the Frog! Richard had another string to his incredibly lengthy bow.

But that was to be my last day in the sun. That very afternoon, Richard had taken Kim, Toni and Linda back home in the Frog. I had tried to squeeze myself in the back seat between Linda and Toni, but after much cajoling and froshing about I found myself by the side of the road with my schoolbag around my head, exhaust fumes up my nostrils, and the green Frog hopping over the horizon. So much for my mate Richard, I thought. So much for having been the best of buddies since Year Nine. For the love of three women, he had cast aside our close, though slightly volatile, friendship. He had sold out on me, damn it! He had sold his soul to women and I was left with nothing but a long walk home.

Over the next few days the situation deteriorated.

For one thing, Billy Loxton was visibly annoyed at Richard's newfound popularity with Sally. Billy decided to up the wheeling stakes and took to riding his own Kawasaki motorbike to school. Sally must have been impressed by his leather boots-and-all performance because I saw them both shoot past the school bus – Sally, her long blonde hair streaming out from underneath her helmet; Billy gripping the handlebars with poise and flair – before some twit in Year Eight hit me on the side of my head with a football. The ball knocked some questions into my melon, like: Why was I just peering out of the window? Why wasn't I out there like Richard and Billy? Why was I sitting in the school bus with the Year Eights and Greg when everyone else in my year charged to school under their own steam? I was a man, damn it. I was old enough to get my provisional licence. I was smart – I had scraped through the learners' test without even studying the drivers' handbook. Driving was simply an application of common sense. For some stupid reason I hadn't gone on to get my provisional licence while everyone else had. Every day that passed, my dreams of romance and popularity were being squashed under the wheels of Richard's amphibiously-named automobile.

So I did what any red-blooded bloke would have done. I secretly dug up my copy of the handbook and studied it hard. I learned how to make a hill start. I read up on the technique for reverse parking. I discovered blind spots. I became acquainted with the accelerator and the brake. I mastered the art of rotating the steering wheel without crossing my hands, in spite of Dad's claims that "I'd bugger the power steering" of the Mazda by practicing whilst parked in the driveway. Sometimes, when Mum and Dad were working in the backyard, I reversed the Mazda out of the driveway and drove it in again to reassure myself that my skills were on the up. On only one occasion did I scrape the letterbox. Dad still thinks that someone must have side-swiped him at the shopping centre.

And when it came to the driving test, I thought I did very well really, especially considering my lack of on-road experience. I didn't hit a single car, even on the reverse park! And I only stalled once on the hill start. On the second attempt I gave the examiner's little car so many revs that we shot up the hill in very smart time indeed. The only thing I *knew* I got wrong was right at the start of the test. Being so nervous about "passing first go" (like Richard claimed he did on *his* test), I forgot to put my seatbelt on. At the first set of red lights, the examiner asked me if I'd like to wear one. He was very nice about the whole thing, and he didn't get annoyed when I missed the green signal while figuring out which lever operated the indicators.

I was pleasantly surprised to be told how many points I'd accumulated, once back at the Motor Registry.

"You're meant to avoid points!" The examiner had rudely explained, before ordering me out of his car. "Come back again when you can change gears. One day you'll appreciate driving in something other than first."

So here I am outside the Motor Registry, depressed, wondering if I should catch a bus or just walk home.

In a way, I'm glad that I failed. If I had passed, Richard and the girls at school would start hassling me about getting a car, I'd be hassling Dad, Dad would be hassling me to get a job to pay for it, and so on. There is so much more to driving a car than impressing girls. Cars are costly. They have to be maintained. Petrol is expensive. So is insurance. The train trip isn't all that bad. I can use public transport to catch up on all the homework I've missed while learning the handbook.

And I can always talk with Greg on the bus from Crookwell station.

Who cares about wheels anyway? There is so much more to life than that, isn't there? All things considered, I just don't think that any girl is worth the bother.

CAREERING

"And then I *knew* that I wanted to be a teacher!" exclaims Greg on the bus.

Oh god. I really hate it when people say gunk like this. Especially on Careers Day. It has nothing to do with wanting to be a teacher. Teachers are bearable. Some teachers are even okay. Rather, it is the awful self-deluded certainty of the speaker which reaches out and sickens you. This person knows what they want to do, damn it, and get out of their way if you don't. It's bad enough when the person making the remark is only in Year Seven. Let's face it, teaching is probably the profession they've come into most direct contact with, and the standard set at Crookwell High is hardly inspirational. But it's downright horrible when you see them six years later, regarding their chosen career with the same, ridiculously excited fervour. How can Greg be so sure of himself? Hasn't he ever grown out of the excitement of living nine-to-five, or at least, nine-to-three? I grew out of it a long time ago: Year Ten, I think.

Everyone in Year Ten was excited about forging a career, even myself for a time. I blame it squarely upon the wild monetary excesses which developed during that year, pre-empting the run on the stockmarket. That was also the year the wheels phase really took off. Before then, only rich show-offs drove to school in their own cars. Then, suddenly, everyone with a bit of spare cash was turning up in whatever rusty contraptions they could lay their hands on. In fact, I think this had a direct influence on Richard's current motoring endeavours. Girls are attracted to those with cars, to those in the money. In Year Ten, the carpark was full of the senior students' dazzling motors – Fords, Valiants, and even the odd Chrysler. To me, these cars came to symbolise the mad consumerist bandwagon which subverted my embryonic thinking nihilism, and temporarily replaced it with a pragmatic, corporate high-flying attitude.

I remember when my nihilism began to wane. I had received my first ever 'A' for a Year Ten Commerce essay. It was entitled "Banking and

Credit Cards". I would have got an A-plus except that I forgot to point out that the three b's in the Bankcard logo actually represented the three sixes of the devil as forewarned in the Revelations of John. Credit and loans were therefore very evil. As a direct consequence, the lord himself would come racing over the hilltop, most likely after the following month's credit statement fell due. This sort of reasoning is commonplace at our school whenever commerce teachers are recruited from Harvey College. But, despite my slight omissions, I felt that my essay revealed a previously hidden ability.

"And then I *knew* I wanted to be a corporate mogul with an Economics/Law degree," I had panted breathlessly to the ancient school careers adviser, Old Ronny Wright, who doubled as the school chaplain. I have always felt uncomfortable around Ronny, especially in Bible class, and I was not accustomed to talking with him about careers. In fact, I have always thought him a bit of a jerk. He is always trying to snap up candidates for Harvey College, or heaven. But Year Ten work experience was coming up, and he was the only person in the school I could see. I wanted to leap into my high-powered career on the right foot.

"So let me get this straight," Ronny had said. "Ever since kindergarten, where you argued for the extension of bank credit to children, you have harboured a desire to become proficient in business and earn 'a great wad of cash', as you put it."

"Yeah."

"It has nothing to do with that essay you're holding to your chest?"

"Oh no, not at all." I placed the scrunched paper in my bag, but not before giving Ronny a surreptitious flash of the grade. "So what do you recommend?"

"Recommend?"

"For work experience! What does a potential mogul do for work experience nowadays? Where should I go?"

Old Ronny scratched his head. "Well, there *is* Harvey College..."

I should have known that Ronny would give me this sort of advice. The man is a walking Bible. Nothing new has entered his head for at least two thousand years. There was absolutely no way that I would be going to Harvey College. All they managed to produce there were ministers and Bible-toting commerce teachers, both of which had incomes considerably below that of your average entrepreneur. No, I was smarter than that, I reasoned to myself, and my logic in Year Ten was impeccable. Girls were attracted to money. I was attracted to girls. I would become a rich entrepreneur. Girls would be attracted to me.

QED.

Over the next few weeks I studied the entrepreneurial form guide. I scoured newspapers and magazines for articles on the richest, most famous and most successful 'winners' of our age. Some of what I learned was quite strange. Many of the top earners were in their fifties and had studied Arts at university, not Law or Economics. Some didn't even have a degree. One had been a signwriter before making enough money to build his own private university. Some talked of joining a firm at the bottom and working their way up to the top. Others talked of starting at the top by borrowing large amounts of money from the bank. Nearly everyone had a tax shelter in the Cayman Islands and a spare house in Spain. It was compulsory to have dined at the Prime Minister's country retreat.

But the most informative piece I read was tucked away in the middle of an obscure magazine, *The Go-Getter,* called "The Language of the Future". It was written by some American who claimed that the path to fortune in the future would be in the computer industry. This made good sense. Business and government could not operate today without modern technology. To control the technology was to control the world. The proof was all around me – our school had bought twenty new computers the previous week for dubious 'educational' purposes. So, after dismissing the idea of becoming a signwriter, I instead signed myself up to spend my two weeks of work experience with a local entrepreneurial computer company.

Upon recollection, I don't think I learned a terribly great deal during my time at Bazza's Computers Incorporated. But so what? Two weeks was far too short a time to become accustomed to peering at the insides of a central processing unit. However, I could smell the air of *potential* in the place. Sure, it was just a grimy garage workshop owned by two ex-mechanics with long beards, gout and foul breath, but it was a start. I felt sure that I had observed the first, teetering steps that led into the world of wealth and entrepreneurship. And this would impress Sally no end. At the time, that had been the most important thing of all.

Sure enough, Sally had pricked up her ears when I told her about the garage. "A garage! That's really cool, Gary," she had beamed.

I reddened in the sudden warmth of her praise and returned similar compliments about her experiences in the fashion photography trade.

"So what cars did you check out?"

I shook my head. "I didn't look at cars..."

"Bikes then. I love bikes. Suzukis? Kawasakis?" Sally looked at me with longing eyes. "Harley Davidsons?"

It was then that I hit her with my big news.

"Actually, the garage was converted into the site for an entrepreneurial computer business. I examined all sorts of computer componentry and electronics."

Sally rolled her eyes. For a moment I thought she had been taking lessons from Jennifer Dukes. "Oh shit Gary! How dweeby!"

"Dweeby?"

"Geeky, then. And to think that I thought you were cool."

Dweeby! Geeky! That 'dweeby' business would be raking it in after a few years. Dweebs like me would be rolling in dough, much more than Billy at any rate. And I told Sally as much. But she just sighed.

"I don't give a stuff about money, Gary. I just like cars and bikes."

Then she wandered off, leaving me alone with the bubblers.

I took a long drink.

Soon after, my nihilism returned.

SUPER-RICH

Now, in Year Twelve, I'm not so uptight and ambitious about careers. My nihilism takes care of that. I'm more concerned about inequalities between the rich and the poor, the have-money and the have-money-nots. There may be a question on it in the Economics exam at the end of the year.

We are initiated into the money club at an early age. And for good reason. Without a pile of fivers or a wadded wallet of tens, it would be very difficult to do anything in life. Like most people, I'll be sentenced to spend my life outside school selling my labour in return for hard bucks so that I can purchase a place to live, food to eat and a programmable video recorder to tape the best bits on the telly while I'm out selling my labour. Those parts of my income that will not be spent on sustaining myself for the day will be saved for tomorrow or the next rainy day, presumably for a good umbrella. As of yet, I still haven't quite got the hang of saving. I need every cent I get to make the most basic of ends meet from the school canteen, and it didn't help that Monaco bars went up ten cents last week. Now the ends don't even come close to meeting. If anything, I think I'm going out backwards.

But is this the same for everyone? I often think that if I had a million dollars, then I'd be okay. I could put the whole kerbang into the bank or some shares and just live off the returns. Once I had a million dollars, there would be no need to work or worry about the world. This would be great. It would leave me more time to ponder the utter meaninglessness of being a millionaire and whether I am truly happy or not. Maybe I could toddle around with a media empire or something.

Yet many people seem to defy the million dollar bliss point. A quick perusal of the Top 100 in *Wealth* magazine reveals the incomprehensibly vast amount of moolah accumulated by those in the upper echelons of Capitalia. This is a list of Western society's new royalty, and even a few of the old ones. These people are not just rich, they're 'super-rich'. The list itself is quite informative, taking away for the moment the fact that many of the super-rich have probably underestimated their wealth by a factor of thirty or so to evade wealth and income taxes. In many respects, it resembles a pop singles chart. There's a column for this year's fiscal position, last year's fiscal position, a star label for bullet performers, and an icon for how many albums (read 'biographies') they've managed to sell.

Climbers. Re-entering the charts at number one hundred is Jacques Saffron, a 'hard-nosed' businessman whose multinational company, Cortek, produces specialist car parts for several leading manufacturers. It says here that he is very happy with the increased productivity of his plant since he 'downsized' his labour force and replaced them with robotics. Presumably humans cost too much in wages and are too lazy to work a twenty-four hour day. His remaining workforce recently won a prestigious European efficiency award – she plans to have a holiday in America to celebrate her prize. If she does, then she will be bound to come across Kurt Powell's casino chain. Kurt's leaped fifteen places on the ladder, thanks to being granted gaming licences in the States in addition to the licences he holds in Canada, Europe and Australia. It isn't a licence to print money, he claims. It's just a licence to offer gamblers a clean, professional betting service. "That's the beauty of capitalism, folks," blares *Wealth* magazine. "Wherever there is a demand, competition dictates a supply!" Jeez! So getting rich is a community service! But I suppose that the editor has to make it sound that way. After all, he *is* employed by Ross Maughan, the astoundingly successful media magnate who sits at number four on the list. Ross owns a large chunk of the 'information sector' – papers, magazines, radio, pay and free-to-air television – as well as several movie studios. He also pioneered 'infotainment' while covering a small war in the Middle East. The ratings success has prompted him to organise other rating 'coups'. I hope his underlings don't take this directive the wrong way.

Sliders. Dropping from twelve to thirty-three is the Queen of England, who, upon filling out an income tax form for the first time, accidentally ticked the box which said "less than 2000", thinking that it was referring to Rolls Royces. Consequently, an appeal has been set up to help Her Ailing Majesty. I'm sure that a lot of prayers will go out to her in these terrible times. There won't be any prayers for the former *Tower of Power* evangelist, Timmy Sailor, though. He had pleaded with his flock to part with their wallets to help build missions in the 'uncivilised' East. Unfortunately for the East, and Timmy, the money never made it to the mission-fields. Most was eventually located in Timmy's bank account. The remainder had helped build several luxury estates for his family – no doubt a pecuniary reward for doing the good lord's good work. Confiscation of these assets by law agencies has pushed the Sailor clan to almost abject poverty: number ninety-seven on the Top 100 list. The same fate has befallen Christopher Chase, who veritably plummeted from the charts and into the Top Ten of the world's worst dressed men. Christopher used to be a player in the leisure and tourist hotel construction industries. However, his company collapsed after failing to meet its debt requirements. If it's any consolation, the Mirage Hotels Consortium was voted the most aptly named commercial enterprise since the international triangular cricket competition was labelled a World Series.

Bullets. Here there is no contest. By far the greatest bullet performer in the Top 100 is Mikey Matterson, the American computer software king, whose personal wealth of over thirty billion dollars has catapulted him into the Top Ten. His money seems to have led a merrily reproductive life over the past twelve months. Mikey was one of those dorks at school who dreamed of making his first million dollars designing operating systems for IBM. When he told girls this, they laughed in his face. Now he's the head of his own software company; a multi-billionaire dork who makes Prime Ministers, Presidents and royalty laugh in his face when he tells them a good joke, or else.

He still can't get girls though.

Thirty billion dollars. That's a terrible amount of money. One billion is one thousand million, so thirty billion dollars comes to thirty thousand million smackers. It is a quarter of the size of the foreign debt owed to banks by South American countries and roughly equal to the amount of money spent on America's nuclear technology research every week. But, apart from building a nuclear warhead or a space station, or purchasing Brazil, what can you do with so much cash? Take away expenses for food, housing, travel and movies from thirty billion dollars and you are left with, roughly, thirty billion dollars. I think, given a little time and creativity, I could spend the interest from one million dollars, but the interest from thirty thousand million? There's not enough time in the day to off-load that much money without lowering the super-rich standard and donating to charities. So I guess it just sits there and accumulates and earns even greater returns.

Mikey and his ilk are riding the perfect wealth wave; they've found the eternal curl. But something inside me knows that it can't last

84

forever. One day so much water will be dragged into the wave that the knife-edge reef below will be exposed. But Mikey will be okay. He's got his board to land on.

I've only got my pair of Speedos.

RUMOURS

Sometimes I wish I were higher up the wealth list.

I usually crave more cash while relaxing in the video arcade next to Sandhurst railway station. I often stop in here for a bit before catching my bus home. *Video arcade.* It sounds weird, doesn't it? I heard that they used to be called pinball parlours. Then the first video game appeared – Space Invaders – and the 'pinnies' became the 'spacies' overnight. That game hooked a generation. But, like today, there was probably always one rich bastard hogging the machine with a line of credits as long as your arm. Space Invaders became so popular that the proprietors bought six stand-up machines and placed them side-by-side along the wall. Their faith was rewarded. A whole new generation of video players became arcade regulars. Pinnies were suddenly out of vogue.

Sure, there was an outcry against the new movement. Concerned parents said that kids were wasting their money playing these games. They said the games were too violent, glorifying aggression and war. It was rumoured that the arcades operated as centres for youth crime and truancy. But worst of all, they said the games were a waste of time. Things haven't changed much since then. Dad *still* reckons that they are a waste of time. But he watches too many sensationalised current affairs programs on the telly – so I don't know how he can lecture *me* about time-wasting. But the truth of the matter is that I don't waste any time in an arcade. I only have a fifteen minute window between the time my train arrives at Sandhurst station, and the time my bus leaves for home. Those fifteen minutes are about the most precious minutes of the day – almost as precious as the time spent dozing on the field during lunchtime – and, generally, I utilise the time as best I can.

The Sandhurst arcade gradually filled up with a whole range of video games. Each new game was more exciting than the last, more challenging, more technically advanced. A small group of diehards kept playing the pinnies up the back of the arcade, but your average spaciejunkie was more interested in blasting the invading aliens from the planet Zercon, preventing nuclear Armageddon on Earth, or travelling through time. And for less than a dollar a pop, such fantastic excursions were within my reach.

Now the bastards have doubled the price, and I sit here contemplating inequality, money and careers – instead of playing the games I love.

Peter Woolley sits down at a World Cup Soccer game just opposite me and starts to play. He is dressed in the traditional Tresham College uniform: tie loosened at the neck, white shirt hanging out underneath the heavy blazer, his crumpled Tresham bag shoved untidily against the legs of the video machine. But the air of reckless abandon seems at odds with his establishment Tresham paraphernalia. He looks unhappy.

He acknowledges my stare with a nod, before plundering another goal against Argentina. Five nil! And still twenty seconds on the clock. Peter is an expert, and he notices my noticing.

"I know a few tricks and tactics to win this game." The corner of his lip curls in satisfaction. "And I've had a lot of practice."

These are the first words he has ever spoken to me. I don't really know how to respond. Should I just act natural? Should I answer him? I've got to say something.

"Could you show me?"

"And lose my mortgage of talent on this game? Sure. Why not?" The words are directed at me, but his face is screwed up in concentration on the screen below. His goalkeeper catches a fierce shot on goal by the Argentinians, and he boots his side into attack once more. His central midfielder parries the ball against his chest, then makes a scorching diagonal run to the right hand corner of the field. A wicked cross follows, which is blasted into the back of the net by his main striker. Six nil. Time up. On to the final against Germany.

"That's the main weapon," explains Peter casually. "You drive the ball up to the corners and cross it back to your strikers, then *wham!* you hit both kick buttons simultaneously for the shot on goal."

"But your striker did a bicycle kick! How did you do that?"

Peter strokes some hair back from his face. "I was a little tardy getting the cross in. My striker overran the ball. If I had timed it properly, he would have used his head. Doesn't matter really."

I nod thoughtfully. "You know, I haven't seen you in this arcade before."

"Usually I'm at the Zone around the corner. But they've got rid of their soccer game because no one except me played it. So now I'm here."

The final is now underway. Peter launches his side into attack, pushing the ball to the left wing to set up a cross, but the German cover forces the play into touch.

"How's Tresham?"

"Huh?" He glances up momentarily, then returns his attention to the game. "What do you think? It's shit. I'm just a faggot day boy. You don't know how good you've got it at Crookwell High. Especially the girls." A German raid on goal results in a corner kick. Peter curses.

"Like Sally you mean?"

A short laugh. "Nah. You've been listening to Greg too much."

"But Greg reckons..."

"It's rubbish." Corner saved. Back into attack. Thirty-five seconds to go. "Believe me, not Greg. He couldn't keep a secret if he tried. That's why I told him about the beach party."

"But what about Sally?"

"Who cares? Look. I just wanted to get up Billy's nose. One thing I really wanted to do before leaving Crookwell High was to get one good shot on that lump of shit. I just wanted him to fight me. We never got along." A sharp break up the right hand side of the field, the expected cross, and a headed goal just inside the left post. One nil.

"And, in front of a school like that, let me tell you: it was worth it. It was worth whatever Billy could throw back at me. I didn't want to leave quietly, as I had always been too damn quiet at Crookwell. I swore that I would go out with a bang."

Go out with a bang? That's exactly what Toni had said on the field that lunchtime! Hell, she had known all along. Peter must have told her about it. So Greg had mistaken Peter's rumour for fact, while Toni had tried to pass off her knowledge of the incident as hearsay and reasoning, and it was nigh impossible for me to differentiate between the two. Fact and fiction are always irrecoverably intertwined at Crookwell High anyway. Every event, every incident, is relayed around the school body like a mass game of Chinese whispers. Knowledge is distorted into gossip, rumour is moulded into reality, reputations are destroyed and others created. It is the complete opposite of everything scholarship and logical, erudite debate stands for. It is exactly what Crookwell High has become.

Peter's gaze interrupts my thoughts. The final has been won in a close contest. "So Toni told you? Well. It doesn't matter now. It was bound to come out in the end. You know what they say: the truth will out."

Will it? Peter had started the rumour precisely to prevent the truth from coming out. And is this really the truth anyway? It's hard to tell. I'm curious as to why he left though. Did he hate Crookwell High that much?

Peter seems to read my thoughts. "I didn't want to leave Crookwell High you know, despite all the crap I copped there. But my parents were worried about my future. They want me to get a high mark in the final exams. They were worried about my attitude too. So they said I had to go to a proper boys school. Just like that. I wasn't given a chance to say what I wanted, how I felt. And I felt pretty pissed off. It was like living in a bad dream for the next week or so. Then the first day of school came round..." His voice fades.

"So you came to Crookwell instead."

"I felt kinda brilliant that day. Crookwell High had nothing over me any more. During my time there as a student, I would never directly cause trouble for the fear of being expelled and sent somewhere else, like Tresham. How's that for irony? Now there was nothing to lose. It didn't matter any more. For the first time in my life, I felt so utterly free." He looks down at his watch. "Shit! Is that the time? I'm going to miss my bus."

I have forgotten about the time as well. We walk out of the arcade together. I feel that we have become comrades, after a fashion.

"Oh yeah, Gary..."

I turn back to face him. "Yeah?"

"Oh, just forget it. It was nothing."

Something tells me it is very important. "Come on. What?"

Peter pauses, almost embarrassed by what he has already said. "Has Toni approached you... uh... said anything to you yet... about anything?"

"Well... what do you mean?" My heart is racing.

Peter waves me away. "No, really. Forget it. I've got to catch my bus. Toni is just one misunderstood, lonely person." He moves off. "I guess we all are."

I stand outside the arcade, the implications of what Peter just said crashing down upon me. Does he mean what I think he means? Is this just another game for him? Another rumour? Does he get his kicks leaving people in dreadful uncertainty? What a wanker! Well, it won't work with me. Toni? And me? Hardly! The idea is completely ridiculous. Laughable! Ha! Ha ha! I can see through Peter's ruse. I'm no

Greg. I don't believe everything I hear. Besides, I have it on good authority from Linda Travers, who got it off Sally, who got it off Richard, who got it off Kim, that Toni isn't interested in my type at all. Like all girls, she isn't interested in deep philosophy and intelligent conversation mixing with her sex life. Nah. She's only interested in those big *Cleo* guys.

BIG

Regardless of what tall people may say, it isn't easy being short. In politically correct talk it means 'vertically challenged, inconvenienced or constrained'. Why else would someone write a song with the lyrics:

> *Short people got no reason*
> *Short people got no reason*
> *Short people got no reason to live...?*

I can't exactly remember how the rest of the song panned out, except to say that the words 'short people' were probably replaced in later choruses by references to other popularly vilified minority groups, such as pensioners or people who spend more than five minutes at automatic teller machines, or both. The tune and lyrics of this particular refrain, however, swirl around in my head all day at school. I even start humming it during Mr White's Economics class.

"Put a sock in it, Gary," recommends Jennifer, threatening to roll her eyes once more. Hell, I can't help it. It's kind of catchy. And true. Well, half true.

It's certainly true for guys. And I should know. I'm always the last in line for class photographs; eventually shoved on the very edge of the frame, just behind the girls who sit in the front chairs. (This makes me appear a little taller.) I've never made the high school basketball team. (Mind you, I've never applied – it's a very stupid game.) And I could never secure the star roles in English drama productions. They were reserved for the protein-saturated members of the class who had 'presence'. This is another politically correct term meaning 'big'. Whether they could act or not was beside the point. Come to think of it, my only appearance in a dramatic production, after being rejected for the plum roles of Algernon in *The Importance of Being Earnest* and Captain Shotover in *Heartbreak House,* was to play the infantile Dill in a challenging theatrical reconstruction of the court scene from *To Kill a*

Mockingbird. My one line was to say "Looky over there, Jem!", which *was* in the script, and then to fall backwards off the school-desk cum jurybox, which wasn't. By all reports, however, I had said my line with the polish and verve of an accomplished thespian. It was just my luck that none of the texts we studied in English had short characters in starring roles.

But the worst of apart-height discrimination manifests itself in my lovelife. Or, more precisely, my current lack of it. Short guys aren't sexy. Short guys are 'dweeby', to borrow a term from Sally. Short guys are not an asset that you can brag about to the popular girl cliques. Short guys have paranoias about being short. And whoever said "good things come in small packages" was speaking bullshit, or, at the very least, has never been a member of the eight-inch club that allegedly congregates behind the cricket nets after school. I swear I'll kill the next person who says it to me. It really shows a lack of knowledge about the human psyche. This psyche demands, to be quite blunt, that it is not good enough to be short and male. All girls like their blokes to be strong, muscular and tall. I don't know why. Perhaps they like to feel protected; who knows what from – perhaps other strong, muscular tall guys. I blame it all on a conservative upbringing.

If you're a short guy, you have to make it up in some other way. You have to go out of your way to fashion an alternative attractive feature. How many times have I heard the same crappy story about the short lad in the class who played the clown to be accepted? Or had to memorise reams of romantic poetry to be sexy? The short guy must always search for his ticket to redemption. And is this tendency reflected in girls? No way, because guys don't really give a rat's arse about height. Jamie Ulcott likes girls with a "lot of leg". I presume by this he means he likes tall girls. Yet Richard likes Kim – and she only reaches his navel! (He says it has its advantages, but when pressed is reticent to reveal them to me.) Heck, us guys could love anyone! I used to like Sally, and she is neither short nor tall. I certainly wouldn't care less if she was shorter or taller. In fact, the thought has never crossed my mind till now. She could definitely lose a few pounds though. And as for Toni... well... that's only a rumour surely?

Last year, while I was hopelessly infatuated with Sally, I had sought the advice of Richard Taylor, the greatest babe-magnet in the school.

"Why don't you do some work with weights?" he had suggested when I told him my dilemma. "In a few months you'll be pulling the babes."

I informed Richard that my problem was not so much *weight,* but *height.*

"Look, man. You'll never be able to improve on your height. Make the most of what you've got. Build up. That's my philosophy."

"But it's just another manifestation of the same problem. Why should looks matter so much? Why can't people see beyond the surface?"

Richard grunted. "Do you have any ugly friends?"

He had a point there. Was I a hypocrite? Well, not really, I thought. I have very few friends to speak of at all – ugly or otherwise. I think I could easily make friends with a lot of ugly people if it were strictly necessary.

But Richard's philosophy of building up became my philosophy when I discovered that Sally had joined the aerobics class for Tuesday sport – and the weight-training options were held at the same fitness centre in North Crookwell. So, viewing the situation in a new light, I decided to give Tuesday afternoon chess with Greg the old heave-ho. I was going to be big, damn it. But in a nice way.

As it happened, several factors were to work against me during that long winter in Year Eleven. Firstly, I didn't want Sally to see my emaciated flesh before the results of the rigorous work-out program. This necessitated the wearing of a large green cardigan to, from and during the routines. Secondly, a couple of rowdy boofheads from 12C who liked using my head as a toilet brush were nominated by the weights master to be my partners. Thirdly, the weights master was none other than Mr Robertson, whom I last had the misfortune to meet by the swing bridge at Harvey College. Fourth, Sally always seemed to enter the room when I was trying to lift fifty kilos on the bench press. Worse, on a couple of occasions, Sally helped by lifting the bar off me when it proved too heavy, or when my cardigan got tangled up in the pulley system. (My alleged partners were perving in the girls' changing room at the time.) Fifth, Mr Robertson decided to take an intimate interest in my personal growth. And finally, most horribly of all, Sally injured her knee in the third week whilst completing a complex starjump manoeuvre and spent the remainder of the term playing chess with Greg.

All my plans had come to nothing and, even after two months of painful, intensive training, my biceps were no bigger than shelled walnuts. Richard's soothing claims that they had doubled in size over the term did little to improve my ailing self-image. I had a lot of serious thinking to do; a lot of questions to answer, like: Why the heck do guys

do this? What is the point of putting your body through sheer hell?
Surely no prize is worth so much effort? I wasn't able to straighten my
right arm for two weeks because of cramps. That was the last time I'd
listen to Richard's refreshing brand of philosophy, and I said as much to
Greg the following term. Guys who work out just to impress girls are
very shallow creatures indeed.

"But some guys don't even work out!" Greg had informed me.
"They're just naturally tall and muscular."

"Oh put a sock in it, Greg."

"Come on Gary. It's not all that bad. Don't you know that good
things come in small packages?"

I thought about it.

I really did.

III
OUT OF TIME

LOVESTRUCK

I have come to the conclusion that it is possible that I am in love with a certain girl at school. She is a few months older than me, is taller than me, definitely more trendy and, judging by the results on our HSC assessments throughout the year, she is also one hell of a lot smarter than me too. That this emotion of mine is not directed at Sally McVey, my childhood sweetheart swing bowler (who never returned my affections anyway), makes for a major turning point in my life, I think. Since losing interest in Sally, I have been drifting in a sort of nowhere land; a land where I had thought I could love nobody and, perhaps more pertinently, I had thought that nobody could love me. I had thought I was free of the love virus forever; free of all the worry and stress that goes with relationships (or at least in contemplating one); free from the (expected) hassle of girls constantly ringing me up, interrupting my study time and the associated meditations prescribed by my stress psychologist; free from the awkward dependency, the empty need; free to philosophise; free to spend my time looking within myself; free to read *Jacko! The Story of a Champion* and listen to my favourite music tapes.

Then I met Peter at the arcade and everything changed.

For some terrible reason, despite my desire to be independent, aloof and focused on my upcoming exams, I find myself succumbing to the virus yet again. Damn it! Just one chink of hope in the rubble of my life, and I'm back to square one. Where is my nihilism now? Why does it matter so much to me that I love and be loved?

I think a lot of it has to do with social conditioning. Love is just one clause in our contract with life. It forms part of our 'purpose': we are all expected to go forth into the world, meet partners, fall in love, procreate, raise a family and die. Those who don't follow the sequence are eyed with suspicion. But just how fair are these conditions? Of course we are all going to die some day, but not everyone should feel as though they have to meet somebody, love somebody, or screw somebody to have participated in Life. But through trashy Hollywood films, pulp fiction, girlie magazines, pop music and commercials for pimple creams, we are continually forced into thinking along these lines. The guys and girls at school who haven't gone out with anybody are viewed with the utmost *contempt:* they're geeks, dags, fags, dykes, dweebs, *losers.* If you haven't had sex by the age of eighteen, you're considered to be frigid, cold or of a Victorian vintage (not to mention a *virgin,* which is bad enough in itself). If you haven't married by the age of thirty-five, you're viewed as *non-committal,* irresponsible, immature – perhaps even a psychotic loner, a potential menace to society. If you choose not to have kids you're eccentric, selfish, sometimes barren or impotent. Our contract with life has firm conditions – breach them and you are an open target for ridicule, pity or scorn.

Yet the clause pertaining to love is particularly dumb when you think about it. I know it's dumb. I've seen lovers and it's not a pretty sight. They were older than me, probably from university, and they had stood opposite from me in the crowded vestibule of the 3:33 Sandhurst-bound train from Crookwell station. While I tried to keep my eyes focused upon my Modern History notes, I could not help but look at these two grown human beings *holding* each other in public. They looked so in love, so happy... and so utterly *brain dead!* I thought to myself: here is a girl who is probably very intelligent, thoughtful and independent, but who now drapes herself over a bloke with the look of a contented cow in a field full of green grass. How demeaning is love! How it drugs us with its warmth. How it removes from us any sense of will, thought or reason. As for the guy, well, he was no better. He held the girl to his chest and gazed, stupidly, out of the train window towards the bowling alley at Berwick. Whether the bowling alley had played a significant role in their courtship I was not sure. Occasionally the eyes of this embarrassing couple would meet, and then the countenances of both would transform so quickly into a state of total bewonderment, that I had to return to my notes on Nazi concentration camps to stop myself from being violently ill.

Yet it wasn't always like this. I used to tolerate lovers when I was in Year Nine. I had to. They were simply everywhere I turned: at school, on the train, on the bus, at the movies, in my sister's bedroom after school, in the pages of the books I read, in the lyrics of the pop music I listened to, and on the telly every night. That I didn't have a lover at the time was no big deal. Judging by love's total invasion into just about every aspect of civil society, I had thought that it was inevitable that I, too, would be lovestruck one day. Sure, I've always had these constant fantasies about facing Sally McVey's inswingers, but that wasn't love. It was just my male hormones playing around. (Or, upon further reconsideration, perhaps it was just a need on my part to show guys like Richard and Greg that I had male hormones to play around *with*. Guys at school get very distrustful if you don't profess to have sexual urges. They think that you're weird, or gay, or both.) Anyway, my real test of love was yet to come, I thought, and so I spent the next few years cautiously waiting for the curse to fall upon me. And what a waste! It has turned out to be three years of nothing! No wonder I had drifted into the nowhere world.

I had just started to feel comfortable living without love, damn it! I was happy to be single, alone. I was glad in the knowledge that I didn't have to please anyone apart from myself. I was grateful that my thoughts weren't dominated by sex, fear and insecurities. I was free of all that extracurricular hassle. For a while, I had contemplated the very purpose of existence. I had objectively analysed the psychology of my peers. I had raised my average mark in Biology from sixty-one to sixty-seven. I had everything sorted out in the run-up to the trial exams. Now my clear understanding is under threat once more.

Even worse, I will be taking someone down with me. If what Peter says is true – if Toni harbours any feelings for me – then I will be responsible for turning an intelligent girl into a mush-headed cow like the one I saw on the Sandhurst train. Our eyes will glaze over into expressions of dull vapidity and we will turn to the obligatory 'lover' activities of walking hand-in-hand through the schoolyard during lunchtime instead of touching up our HSC assessments in the library, writing smoochy letters during Maths class instead of memorising trigonometry formulae, and reading romantic poetry during English instead of perusing Emily Dickinson, Kenneth Slessor and the increasingly handy *Brodie's Notes*. The effect upon our final grade will be disastrous. All the work we have put into the HSC will be undone. We will both miss out on university, fail to get jobs, and end up as part of the city's homeless population, sleeping on park benches during cold winter nights, relying on private charities and government handouts to see us through each day, eventually dying alone, unnoticed by the world, and buried in unmarked graves.

But heck, I think I love her. And that's what counts, right?

MOVES

"No way! *You've* got to make the moves."

Richard's pronouncement is met with eager approval by the other guys in my lunchtime sexual strategy session. All except me, that is. Greg, Jamie Ulcott and some ring-in from 11B who claims to have gone all the way with Rhonda Oljenik of 10W all nod their heads sagely. I turn away in disgust.

I expected as much from Richard. Just because he had made some frankly obvious passes at Kim which secured their partnership, he thinks he knows all about female psychology. What is worse, he thinks that the tactics he used for Kim are applicable to me and Toni. I know differently, of course. Ours is an *intellectual* relationship, not a shallow, physical free-for-all. If I came on to her during PE like a blundering oaf on heat and said "Hey babe, cute arse!" any interest she has in me would evaporate faster than Sandhurst's chances of making the finals without the skills of the mercurial Jacko. Actually, PE wouldn't be a good time for me to say anything. Those classes are best avoided right now. I always look less attractive in my tight yellow tee-shirt and Dunlop sneakers. In any case, I'm still amazed that the line worked so well for Richard back in Year Nine. Only someone who is extremely confident or supremely unconcerned about the outcome could get away with such a crude opener. Perhaps the women's movement had not caught up with Kim at the time. I just can't take the risk that it hasn't caught up with Toni in Year Twelve.

I face the circle. "Okay. Suppose I do make the first move. What do I say to her?"

Richard shrugs. "Hey babe, cute..."

"No. I can't say that."

"It worked for me."

"And she *has* got a cute arse."

"*Jamie!*"

"Shut up, Greg. You should always try to compliment a girl given a chance."

This is getting out of hand. I rub my chin, trying to give everyone present the impression of deep thought. "Somehow, I don't think that Toni will take that as a compliment, Jamie. Not from me at any rate. I think she will expect something a little more meaningful."

"How about writing to her?" adds the ring-in.

"What? Send her a card?" Yes! That seems more like it to me. Less risky. But the other guys frown on the idea.

"You can't do that, man," explains Richard. "You've got to face her, man-to-woman like. No cards, no letters, no phones. Just you and her. If you want her to take you *seriously*."

"So what do I say then?"

"You say that you like her a lot," says Greg. "And that you think she is a very nice person whom you respect very much, and that would she allow you the honour of going with you, while you bend down on one knee and hand her a large bouquet of red roses..."

We all stare at Greg in disbelief.

"I'm not proposing *marriage*, Greg."

"Well, I tried it with Linda."

"You proposed to Linda?"

"Only for going together. Not marriage of course." He forces a laugh.

"So what happened?" asks Jamie.

"She said no..."

"So there goes that line of attack," decides Richard. "You know, Gary, I still think you should say what I said to Kim. All girls are basically the same when it comes to pick-up lines." He stands up and stretches his arms. "Look man, they know it's just a pick-up line. They don't take the line seriously, only your interest in them. They're usually flattered that you've noticed them, even if they act all offended. You've just got to learn to be *cool,* that's all."

"And she *has* got a cute arse."

"*Jamie!*"

"Shut up, Greg."

This sexual strategy session I organised is getting me nowhere. I am surrounded by fools and imbeciles. They just don't realise that I cannot afford to make the first move with Toni. She will turn me down. The words will all come out wrong. She will take everything the wrong way, and I will be out on my arse for sure. Besides, whatever happened to the feminist revolution? It's in all the papers that the white middle-class male empire is in decline. Great! Let the women (wimmin, womyn or whatever) take control. I don't want power. Actually, I don't think that I've ever *had* power, so it's probably easier for me to be a feminist than most guys. Well, if it were up to me, the first thing I'd hand over to the new order would be the patriarchal 'first-mover' advantage. Us males have dominated this decidedly awkward stage of the relationship for far too long already, and it is time for the girls to empower themselves. But they don't! It's so bloody typical! They take the fruits of the sexual revolution, but they choose to ignore the responsibilities that go along with them. And what's a guy like me to do? If I try to crack on to Toni, she might think that I'm being an overly-aggressive male chauvinist pig, denying her the power to make her own choices regarding her sexuality. Yet if I don't make a move, she might think that I don't like her at all and she will lose whatever interest she has in me. The choice between being pro-active or reactive is really no choice at all. I'm doomed either way.

So the best course of action for me to take is the one which results in the least amount of personal damage. No use hurting Toni's feelings *and* getting rejected simultaneously. It's better that I don't ask her at all. This is the logical approach.

"Well, don't look now," says Richard smugly, "but isn't that Toni sitting over by the tennis courts? Alone?"

My spirits surge, then crumble. Yes, it is. Damn. I can't do anything now. I have already decided that my best option, as always, is to do nothing. But the others are not aware of my choice.

"Here's your big moment, Gary, my man. Get in there!"

I feel afraid.

"Do it now, Gary," says Jamie. "Get it over and done with. We'll be backing you up from here."

"Go to her," adds Greg in a ridiculously pedantic tone.

Facing this brainless barrage of blokedom and brotherhood, I stand up and, with much cheering, meat-headed whistles, cries and shouts, set off in the rough direction of Toni. I cannot describe the range of emotions coursing through me as I trudge the terrible distance across the grassy field to the tennis courts. (Though, to be honest, I mainly feel embarrassed, depressed, anxious and sick to the stomach all at once.) My lack of concentration nearly proves to be my undoing, however, when a speedy Year Ten girl intercepts a pass in the lunchtime touch football game and barrels me over in her haste to score. I pick myself up from the altercation, dust down my grey Crookwell High pants, slightly worse for wear, apologise to the referee, Mr Pollard, and continue along my chosen path without any further incident taking place.

"Hi Toni." I drop down next to her, trying hard not to seem particularly fazed by my journey.

"Oh, hi Gary. Nice tackle. But isn't it meant to be touch football?"

"Yeah, well, I didn't even know I was playing. It's fairly hard to cross that field during a footy game."

"Uhuh." She reaches over and brushes some grass and several small sticks from my school jumper. "So what's with all the cheering and whistling over there?" she asks. "Are you all barracking for the Year Ten team?"

Across the field I can see Richard inserting a finger from one hand into a hole shaped by the other. Jamie and the ring-in are shouting raucously. Greg has left for the tuckshop. I decide to risk everything.

"Actually Toni they are all thinking that I have come over here for the specific purpose of asking you out for a date because you see I especially organised them all to be there as the major studs of the school well the ones I know at any rate though I guess you couldn't call Greg a stud to offer me advice and support in helping me to secure your hand in date-dom and of all the talent I assembled the only help I got from them was to say that I think that you have a cute arse or some such but I didn't think that you would like that very much at all so I'm not going to say it."

The words gush from my mouth like the silted run-off from Rundle Dam after a particularly wet month. And my throat had been so dry a few minutes earlier!

Toni stops picking at my jumper. "So you *don't* think I have a cute arse!"

I try in vain to read her thoughts. Is she upset with me? Did I say something wrong? She looks very serious.

"Ahh... I think you have a very nice arse. Very nice indeed. But only if you *want* to have a nice arse, that is. Umm... Err..." Christ! What am I saying? What would the feminist revolution think? What does Toni think?

BRRRRRRRING!

Thank god! It is the bell for fifth period. I dash from the tennis courts to the security of the senior boys' lockers. In all my life, I have never felt so relieved to hear that old bell, even though it signals yet another Bible class under the dubious auspices of Old Ronny Wright.

RAGE

A long time ago, when video recorders came in Beta and the ozone layer was generally where it was supposed to be, the word 'rage' described someone that was in a state of violent frenzy. Now, depending on which party or concert you crash, it means much the same thing. Who will ever forget the Slam Jam Four, who, in a collective moment of intimate one-ness with the bass riffs of Sledge from *Dead Bone,* jumped from the concert stage into the delirious arms, legs, elbows and kidneys of the audience below? Or the ill-fated McIntyre twins from Crookwell High who tried a copycat performance at Berwick a week later?

"Ragers. They were real ragers," Toni had said after the funeral. "They never knew when too much of a good thing was just too much of a good thing."

Then again, everyone is a rager to Toni. Even me. I have tried to explain to Toni in the past that I have never been a rager, been near a raging rave party, or even had a fit of rage, but it makes no difference. For Toni, to be a rager is, I guess, to be human. She never believes me when I tell her, of course. It is inconceivable to her that people exist in the world who don't go out raging every Friday night.

"I can't dance," I explain lamely to her. It's Friday afternoon. We're walking through the queue for the bus back to Crookwell station. Queue-jumping is one of the privileges of being a school senior. I don't know why we are granted the honour. I'm pretty much against elitist privileges in the main. And it's not as though I get home any quicker to resume my HSC study. As if I'd want to study on the weekend.

"Who can dance?" Toni replies. "Nobody really cares. You shouldn't be so self-conscious. You've just got to let the rhythm bounce you around a bit." She smiles, almost nervously, I think. "Look Gary, you never come out. Why don't you come out with us tonight? I know where this great rave is going to be held. You'll like it."

I shift into panic-mode. "'Go out'? 'Rave'?" Is she asking me out for a date? Is she initiating some sort of 'first move'?

"I'm asking you out for a date, you clown." She pauses. "Richard told Kim that you... might be interested if I asked you. It's quite strange, really. He thinks *you* tried to ask *me* out last week, when you said that I didn't have a cute arse."

"I... uhh..."

"So what do you say?"

I hear voices arguing in my head. My nihilist nature is trying to tell me that there is no point in accepting her offer. But Toni smiles beautifully. Her teeth are so white. She has a dimple on her left cheek. Hell, she's nice. My gut reaction tells my nihilist nature to go fuck itself for a change. Oh yes! *Yeah!* For once I seem to be getting somewhere! Still, it is a strange thing for my gut reaction to do. I have trained it to keep its opinions to itself, especially rude ones, and never to get in the way of an executive decision arrived at by my logical, thinking nihilism.

"Okay. Count me in."

The rest of the journey home is fairly uneventful. After dinner, I shower and change into a pair of black jeans. I have no decent tee-shirts of my own, so I decide to borrow Sarah's black *Dead Bone* top. I slip on my matching white Dunlops as the *coup de grâce,* and wait for the others to come and pick me up. Just after nine o'clock, Richard's Frog appears in the driveway and I'm out through the front door.

"Have a nice time," calls Mum from the verandah. "Don't be in too late."

"We won't Mrs Kendall," lies Richard. Then, to me: "Gary, jump in the back. Toni, move over and let him in."

Toni complies and I slide inside beside her, shutting the door behind me. "So, where to now?"

"Coffee in Sandhurst first," says Kim, using the rear-view mirror to apply her lipstick. She smacks her lips approvingly. "Then Preston for the rave."

I glance at my watch. "Why not Preston now? It's quite a drive away."

Toni jabs my side with her elbow. "Don't be silly, Gary. The rave doesn't start for hours yet. We've got the whole night ahead of us."

Richard starts the car and we drive off into that night. I'm a little nervous with Toni so close to me. She is wearing this unbelievably short skirt over a lycra bodysuit. I can see almost up to her hips. I spend the time in the car and at the café in Sandhurst trying not to look as though I'm looking.

It is about twelve-thirty, Saturday morning, by the time we reach the old barn at Preston, scene of this week's raging rave party. But I'm okay, having taken a fair dosage of No Doze with the coffees I'd drunk in Sandhurst. The place is already thumping with music. Bright strobes light the barn's entrance into a carnival of colour. It looks like we are entering Disneyland. At any moment I expect to see Mickey Mouse on speed come hurtling out through the large barn door. A worrying thought occurs to me. It's only a couple of months before the HSC exams, and what we are doing could result in expulsion if Deputy Kelly ever finds out: drinking, dancing and smoking – and on the Sabbath too! It is all so completely evil.

"Come on Gary. Let's go. You only live once." Toni leaps from the car. She looks absolutely stunning. I, rather worryingly, only look myself. But she's right about living once. Stuff the school. Stuff Kelly. I emerge from the Frog.

Inside, it is hot, moist and very noisy. It doesn't take Toni long to size up the dancefloor and drag me into a suitable position.

"Now what?" I shout above the music.

"Just let go and *rage!*" She flaps her arms and legs about in a whirly-burly of energy and excitement, and I let fly a little myself. After a few drinks, plus some curious carcinogens, I begin to settle into a rhythm of sorts and my thinking nihilism returns to hassle me. I start to ask myself thought-provoking questions, like: What the hell am I *doing?* Why am I here? What is it all for? I hate this music. It's entirely against my nature. Am I doing this to be popular with Toni? Am I trying to entrap Toni into some sort of sexual rendezvous by pretending to be something that I am not? Is this what all dates are like? I'm hardly reaching her on an intellectual level. Damn it, it's all so clichéd. Every time the story is the same. Guy wants girl. Guy takes girl out. Girl rejects guy at first, but by making a persistent arse of himself and pretending to be cool, the rendezvous is eventually achieved. Or is this just the way that guys think? Or is it just the way that I think? Is it both? Or is it neither? The music and alcohol is making my head swim. The only things that I can focus upon are Toni's perfect breasts oscillating hypnotically in front of me from underneath her lycra bodysuit. By god, she's beautiful. I think I'm in love. I think I want her. I think... Oh no... I think I've had too much to drink... Oh no... I think I'm going to be sick!

Toni notices the panicky look in my eye. "Is anything up?"

"No. But it's about to be." I dart through the barn, desperately trying to find an exit. I feel so terrified being jam-packed, shoulder to shoulder, with three hundred oblivious ragers, feeling the onset of regurgitation. My stomach suddenly feels strangely empty. Oh shit! It's on its way. My throat and facial muscles contract into the lockjaw position. I search, increasingly panic-stricken, for an out-of-the-way place to drop my load. Then I lose control. A vile concoction of No Doze, coffee, nachos, rum, Crown Lager, peanuts, scotch and Coke erupts like a hot geyser from my throat all over the floor. Some particularly large chunks splash against another rager. I tense up, expecting a fight, but the rager doesn't really notice. He just brushes his hair back into place and continues to stomp with some other guys.

While staring at the mess on the floor, it strikes me that late nights at home with a couple of videos and a pizza have a lot going for them. Suddenly I have this urge to be at home again, away from this throbbing, pumping, sweaty crowd. Where is Toni? Richard? Kim? Oh heck. I've got to go. I turn and flee the barn.

It's cool outside and the air revives me somewhat. I wander the streets around Preston for an eternity. I try calling a taxi, but the lines are all engaged. Hell, it *is* Friday night. Yet I can't go back to the barn. I can't let Toni see me like this. I sit down by the side of the road to think.

"Hey!" A man pulls up beside me in a van. A small child sits in the front passenger seat. "You look a little lost. Do you need a lift somewhere?"

"Where are you going?"

"Sandhurst."

Thank god! A miracle! I'm saved! "Could you drop me off near Glendale?"

"Yeah, sure. Hop in."

Mum has always warned me not to accept lifts from strangers, but this man looks decent enough. And he *has* got his kid with him. Surely I won't be in any trouble? I accept his offer. He opens the sliding door on the side. I sit down amongst a pile of magazines and shut the door.

"Anywhere in Glendale in particular?" He starts the engine and we move off down the road.

"Oh, if you could drop me by the shops, I can walk."

"Sure."

This guy is really nice. The van accelerates to an appreciable speed, and I start to relax. I think about all the problems I've left behind. I really like Toni. Hopefully she won't mind my leaving the rave a little early. And although I'll do anything for her, this will be the last time I'll go raging. Raging isn't my scene. I'm just not the raging type. She'll have to accept me for what I am – a non-party animal. I bundle some magazines in the back of the van to form a crude seat. The front page catches my eye: "What *The Family* can Offer You". *The Family?* Haven't I heard about them? Aren't they some kind of... sect?

The boy in the front seat turns to me and smiles.

KISS

Question 2 *Writing Task* (Allow approx. 20 minutes for this part) Kenneth Slessor, in his poem 'Five Bells', recalls the entire life of a friend in the time it takes to ring a ship's bell. Now write, in any style you wish, about a situation where someone has an out of time, or body, experience. (10 marks)

Question 2 Response

Writing Task: Gary Kendall, 127.

The Kiss

'Schlooping proboscises;
Ensconsulating puce
Of swishing gastronomic utensils
And the swirling of translucence-spit.'
(Or so I vicariously imagined.
And the boys all reckoned
That I was pretty close to the
Mark.)

But 'Yuk!' said one systematically appalled
By the sounds I had mentioned in the old
school hall.
'If kissing were so bad
Then why are we so mad
To get with a girl at all?'

'Well it all just depends' said another boy
morose,
'In the position that you want to place your
lips and your nose.

And how that all relates
To the spaces on her face
And in the throes of the pose that you chose. '

Then he drew a stencil with a pencil or a pen
About the placement of the hands and the
timing when
One should be feeling numb
Enough to remove the tongue
Without a line of spittle stretching tense.

I left then.
More worried than before.
I was not structured like them.
My thoughts came in
Fits and
Starts and
Lists.
And I would never so endure with the lore
Of the kiss.
So, my mind amiss,

I reached the gate and swung it wide
Open
And walked away;
Out to the station
To catch my train.

Inside my stomach
Began to broil
When passing Plaza I saw her
And she saw me...
The rager boy; a mortal coil.
'Sprung unintentionally
From Preston
With The Family,'
I stammered.
My heart hammered.
'Could you still like me?'

And then, oh joy! her brow furrowed,
And creased into forgiving shape.
No words were spoken.

The world slowed
And then
Stopped
Dead.
There was no feeling in my brain.
There were no sounds of car or train,
Or seagulls missed,
That flew past the rail-bridge overhead,
As she leaned forward
For the kiss.

And all the words that I had versed
To those three boys in Old School Hall
Made no sense now
In this timeless world.
This shopping mall.
This universe.

My heart greets dawn from a Parisian café.
My mind soars above Vienna.
My soul dives deep into clear Alaskan waters.

But my tongue; my tongue a-swirl;
My salivical sluice-gate spittle-sausage
Remains in Crookwell
With the Plaza girl.

R

It's astounding what you can pick up and read at a newsagency nowadays. When I was four or five I used to get *Disneyland* comics. As I have grown older, my horizon has broadened towards more demanding journals such as the *Phantom* comics, *Superman* or the *Herald.* But today, right next to the pile of *Heralds,* I'm startled to see a stray edition of *Playboy.*

A gorgeous woman stares back at me from the glossy cover, wearing little more than a wink and a smile and a black lace nightie. She looks me up and down and says: "Pick me up. Have a peek. Go on. Don't be shy. Are you a man or what? Real men buy *Playboy.* I have very large breasts."

Her comments draw considerable ire from the far more erudite edition of *Penthouse,* once I locate it further down the aisle. "Don't listen to her, Gary. She's speaking a load of crap. Only repressed schoolboys buy *Playboy.* You're not one of those are you? You're not like that. No, I can see that you're a fairly sensitive guy. Sensitive guys always blush whenever they see me." Ms October grabs a warm coat from the cover of *Country Living,* wraps it around herself, and then sits down on the edge of the stand.

She lights up a cigarette. "You dream a lot, don't you Gary?"

I shrug my shoulders. Sure I do. I'm doing it now, aren't I?

"I thought so. I've seen your kind a lot around here. No confidence. No experience whatsoever. And it's only your inexperience which makes you nervous about girls, right?"

Yes. That seems right.

"So you become so nervous that you can't ask anyone out. You screw up any dates you get. You rationalise to yourself afterwards that you didn't like the party anyway, that you prefer being alone. You even start telling yourself that you find the idea of love and romance to be stupid, and that physical intimacy is overrated."

So?

"That's too bad, Gary." A long trail of smoke drifts from her nose. "But the worst is when you start fantasising! Like that poem you wrote for the English trial exam. You've got a wild imagination there, but that's not the way to go. No, you have got to tackle your problems head on."

So what do you recommend then?

Ms October grins and extinguishes the butt of her cigarette against an *Inside Sport* magazine. "We've got to go back to the beginning. Your main problem is that you're inexperienced. Hell, we were all innocent at one time or another. It's nothing to be worried about. But I can help. I can show you everything you need to know about sex, privately, in the comfort of your own room – all the things that your parents and your school were too slack to show you. After flicking through my pages, you'll be prepared for anything. If you buy me, I'll transform you into a fully-fledged sex stud!"

Really?

"You've just got to trust me on this one." Ms October removes her coat and reassumes her cover pose. "Anyway, back to work. Oh Gary, by the way, I have even larger breasts than anyone in *Playboy.*"

She has a point there. I tremble. My hand reaches out to the magazine, brushes against its smooth cover, but falls down by my side. I just can't do it. There is something quite dreadful about purchasing porn from a newsagency. An impassable stone wall rises up before me – a craggy remnant of my early moral upbringing. The man at the counter will no doubt leer at me and think "Jeez, another pervert". His wife will probably think I'm a rapist. Not only that, but according to the laws of society, I'm not old enough to buy them anyway. They are rated X or R or something. Conservative, paternalistic laws such as these don't stop the other bods at school though. Toni and Kim are always gaping over mags like *Cosmopolitan* or *Cleo* during lunch and these are fairly pornographic. Nothing but articles on sex, wangers, and pictures of allegedly sexy guys with big wangers. I know, because I read my sister's. Not that it worries me of course. Hell no. Guys are just the same. Richard has a most revealing portrait in his locker of a couple engaging in some sort of nude twister competition. Greg would no doubt find it distasteful – almost evil – if he ever saw it, but Richard only shows it to those with an appreciative eye. Anyway, if Greg saw it, all hell would break loose and sooner or later Deputy Kelly would find out about it. They go to the same church.

I really don't know why people get offended by seeing a naked body. I mean, we've all got one. Do these bods ever look in the mirror after taking a shower? Come to think of it, do these people ever have sex at all? It must be hard to engage in the odd horizontal jog without seeing the evil, naked flesh of your partner. Perhaps they only do it in the black of night with all the lights turned off. Kinky.

Censorship of sex is plain dumb. If anything, the strict taboos only increase my interest when I come across a *Playboy* or *Penthouse.* There is an element of risk here. Danger. Rebellion. So what if the newsagent thinks I'm a pervert? So what if Kelly comes across a racy picture of Ms October in my locker? So what if I'm underage? Heck, I'm not underage at all. I read somewhere (probably in *Girlfriend*) that the human male reaches his sexual peak at the age of eighteen. What's the point of buying *Penthouse* after you've passed your peak? The law's an ass. I'm a real bloke. I have urges. What's wrong with it? I'm not going to rape the first woman I see on the street because of it. These women weren't forced to take their clothes off. It's not exploitative. Girls read *Cleo* and do I complain? No. It's important to discuss sex openly. It's a free world. What the heck. I'll take it.

"Just the *Herald,* thanks."

I pay the money and race out of the store. Yes, it is the old *'Penthouse*-in-the-*Herald'* trick. Thank god they make the *Heralds* so damn big. I am a shoplifter, no less; a petty crim. There is a small pang of regret. I haven't stolen anything since Grade Four when Kim dared me to take a chocolate Freddo from the corner store.

Now I seem to be breaking all the rules.

I walk home, sneak inside the front door and place the magazine under my mattress. I'm not sure how I'm going to keep it hidden from Mum and Dad, but I'll cross that bridge when (and if) I come to it. Eventually the day draws to a close. Mum cooks a roast, which I gulp down like never before. Then, cunningly, I complain of feeling tired and worn out. My parents offer raised eyebrows as I trudge up to my room, but it goes no further. Once inside, I tear off my clothes, put on my pyjamas, lock the door and dive into bed. After a few moments of fumbling under my mattress, Ms October joins me. We are alone at last.

I switch off the light.

I feel so liberated flipping through the *Penthouse* under my bedsheets; the torch aglow, the door locked, the curtains drawn. There is no doubt about it. I have been shielded from sex for far too long. I can feel my guilt and shame washing away. I am now a member of the human race. Until today, my knowledge of sexuality has been, to be frank, quite limited. But Ms October has been right all along. This *Forum* section makes me feel like a walking Kama Sutra! I'm definitely feeling more confident. I turn to the articles. It's amazing! It appears as though I'm not the only bloke who worries about the number of times I masturbate, the size of my wanger, or why it sort of sticks straight up (even recursive on good days) instead of pointing straight out like a windsock. Nor am I alone in favouring oral sex before intercourse, or in being unable to locate the clitoris without a fairly strong hint. Furthermore, other blokes have the same sort of fantasies I have, although I have never imagined doing it with a radical cult member who demands to be deflowered in a pagan fertility ritual that necessitates the use of electrical kitchen appliances. The sort of people that live in Rundle! But it is still very reassuring.

But most of all, I see now that sex is a beautiful thing; the ultimate expression of love between two caring adults. It is neither wrong nor disgusting, and is enjoyed by thousands of people across the world every second of every day.

I've also learned that Ms October has great tits.

F * * * !

It takes a lot to offend a nihilist like myself. Once you have decided that nothing is absolute; that the basis of everything is made of quicksand rather than concrete; that life is utterly meaningless, the trivial notion of *offence* tends to drop out of the picture. In this respect, it always surprises me how people allow themselves – with almost masochistic pleasure – to be affronted. Morals crusaders (wherever they derive their morals from – more often than not from a two thousand year old book written by incensed rednecks and homophobes) attack other members of the community for breaking a moral code which they observe and the others do not. Certain elements of society are easily outraged to learn of sex between consenting teenagers. They moan and wail whenever they read about homosexuality or further immigration in the press. They phone up radio and television switchboards in droves when they hear a so-called 'obscenity' mouthed on air.

Just ask the legendary Jacko.

Jacko was crucified in the daily rags for saying the magical four letter word beginning with 'f' and ending in 'uck' or some such in a live radio broadcast, and not even his impressive efforts for the Sharks could save him from the ensuing tide of wowserish indignation. This just goes to show that being a sporting hero gets you nowhere when you're in a real scrape, especially if the incompetent management of the Sandhurst Sharks is involved. No wonder I didn't get too involved with the game myself, or any other game for that matter, although I don't mind participating as a fan. However, Greg reckons that Jacko is a 'rough, foul-mouthed jock' – not to mention overrated as a footballer – and that he couldn't help but let one horrible obscenity slip through every now and then. Of course, I don't share his point of view. Jacko is a damn fine halfback and one of Sandhurst's best ever captains. Heck, he's a dead-set legend! But Greg doesn't agree.

"Come on Gary!" he whispers while Ms Amy French hands back the English trial papers. "The man's a moron."

I push Greg and Jacko out of my mind. I need an exceptional mark for English. The trial exams are turning out to be the stuff of nightmares. My marks in all my other subjects have slipped badly. I need more than my regular fifty-eight from Ms French if I'm going to be in a position to matriculate.

"Kendall?"

"Here." I pluck my paper from her hand. Greg is almost as anxious as me to find out my mark. He leans over me while I flick through the sections. Bloody ranking system. Jeez! It really annoys me.

I hold the paper close to my chest and glance downwards. Reading Task: sixty! Shakespeare: fifty-eight. Hmmm. Writing Task: thirty.

Thirty?

Thirty?

Surely it's meant to be eighty? But no. The comments give it all away: *Crude and stylistically void. Try to establish a more coherent structure and rhyming pattern. Avoid humour. Above all, try to relate your writing to the question involved. 3/10.*

"Give me a look," pleads Greg.

That's it! "Oh fuck off for once in your life." I'm as angry as hell. Damn it! I had invested fifty minutes of the two hour exam on the writing task alone, and all I get in return is *three out of ten,* with a comment that my poetry is *stylistically void?* Fuck! Ms French's brain *is* a void. Greg has managed to get eight out of ten for a story in which he dies and goes to heaven to meet god. How fucking typical. My poem, 'Kiss', is much more original. Fuck! It is the best piece of fiction I have ever written. I deserve better than this! I deserve more than the lowest rank in the class. My future is on the line. "Fuck! Fuck! Fuck! Fuck!"

Greg holds his ears and turns a trifle white.

I observe him casually. "Oh come on Greg! No one gets that offended by someone saying 'fuck' nowadays. Grow up."

Greg just sits there.

"Fuck. Fuck. Fuck. Fuck. *Fuck...*"

I am just starting to enjoy myself when I feel a tap on my shoulder.

"...Fuck. Fuck. Fuh... Oh *fuck.* Ms French! Ah, funny weather we're having isn't it? Really funny. Funny. Funny. Funny. You know, I was just telling Greg here about the weather..."

"I think you had better see Mr Kelly, Gary."

Oh fuck. There is no point arguing. She caught me cold. The class falls silent as I make my way to the door. I turn back and glare at Greg for good measure before tramping down the stairwell to the Deputy's office. It's so unfair! I wasn't swearing at Ms French. I swear I was swearing at Greg. That's different. Greg needs to loosen up. He can't go through life being so uptight. The world will just look upon him as a turdy wowser. It's too late for Ms French though. The world *already* views her as a turdy wowser. I certainly do.

How can four letters get me into so much trouble? Richard's really cool about swearing. He used to go to Huxley High where everyone swears their arses off, apparently, even the teachers. He told me a story of how his former English teacher blew up when he wrote 'frig' in a creative writing piece. "It's not 'frig', Taylor, it's 'fuck'. Only American conservatives write 'frig'. Would you say 'frig' if you were that character? Be realistic, for fuck's sake. If you write 'frig' again I'll give you a fucking 'F' of my own." That's what his teacher had said. That English class sounds pretty good. I wish I were there. My talent would be respected. I can't even get away with 'damn' in my stories. I have to use 'darn' instead.

When it comes down to it, words like 'fuck' or 'shit' are just combinations of letters; just a sound made with our lips and tongue. How do people get offended by this? It doesn't hurt anyone. It's offensive to smack someone out (to the smackee at any rate, if not to the smacker). It's offensive to kill, make war, or follow Rundle in the football. But god knows how pronouncing a series of letters is offensive. If everyone were brought up not to give a damn about what people say, then swearing would not be an issue. Neither would talk-back radio. A lot of needless hatred, hurt and pain would be eliminated in both cases. And the benefits of having a word like 'fuck' used in everyday parlance cannot be exaggerated. It's a great word, so adaptable. Sure, when said loud and brash it tends to express anger ("FUCK!"), but by lowering the pitch to a breathy whisper it can also indicate amazement, awe, sorrow or concern ("Oh maaate, *fuuu*ck!"). Obviously it can be used as a verb, but it's also a great noun; short, staccato and succinct: "you silly fuck". It can be used as an adjective: "you fucking fuck"; indeed, as just about anything really: "didn't give a flying fuck", "fucked in the head" or "fucking-well fuck off you fucker, you fucking fuck of a fuck". Come to think of it, if people weren't so easily offended by swearing, then non-English speaking tourists and the like could learn half the language in one word. They probably know it already. Imagine! No more spending weeks with language audio tapes and videos. The world would become a more closely-knit community.

I reach Kelly's office. The door is open. The Deputy lurks inside.

"Kendall. Come in please, and shut that door behind you."

I don't think that Mr Kelly will share my liberal philosophy about swearing. Not that I care much any more. I've got the exams to worry about, and a girl, whom I think I love terribly, to be told that. I've got to get her. I've got to invite her to the Formal. There is so much to do before the final exams, before my time at Crookwell comes to an end. Anyway, the usual penalty for the heinous crime of swearing is either a brief suspension, an afternoon detention, or thirty-two demerit points, although it is rumoured that one bod in the past was expelled for calling the school a 'fucking hell-hole'.

Yeah, forget about swearing. It's the truth which always hurts the most.

FRAUDS

Life can be kind. Life can be cruel. It can be annoyingly self-righteous about its impartiality. Is life unpredictable? Maybe. Crazy? Certainly. Stupid? It seems so. Life is blind to our feelings – dispassionate, savage and violent at one moment, pathetic or pithy the next. It doesn't pretend to operate on any inherent moral code. 'Bad' people are not treated any worse or better, on average, than the 'good'. The 'worthy' will not always prevail. The 'truth' will not always out. Things do not come to those who wait. Early to bed and early to rise does not make you healthy, wealthy or wise. Slow and steady will not win the race. Life is more random, more *chaotic* than this. It cannot be explained through the application of simple, hard and fast rules. In fact, the only constant I can find in this whole life thing is that, to some small extent, some particularly nasty effects seem to follow from certain causes. For instance, if I were to pick a fight with Billy Loxton, life would generally dictate that I would get my head smashed in. Or, more pertinently, if I were to swear at Greg in front of Ms French, I might very well find myself spending my last two weeks of school lunchtimes cleaning windows and furthering my education in the workings of chain-flush toilet systems.

Today is my last day on detention.

I wipe a circle of grime from the large pane of glass at the rear of the library and look down on to the field below. My dubious peers are engaged in that most peculiar event in the HSC calendar: Year Twelve Muck-Up Day. Outrageous! This is the one time of the year where rebellion is sanctioned by the proper authorities. Even Greg is joining in the annual revolutionary traditions of egg-tossing, honey-painting, exhaust-pipe popcorn loading and other assortments of organised subterfuge and villainy. No demerit points are scheduled for today. *Hypocrites!* Richard grabs Kim and shoves a fistful of itching powder down the back of her shirt. She screams in pleasure before beating a hasty retreat to the senior girls' lockers. Billy Loxton has Greg in a headlock. Jamie Ulcott is talking with Toni. *Get out of it. She's mine, kiddo.* It's true, sort of. She's coming with me to the Formal at least. Richard and I are checking out formal hire this afternoon after school. I was quite the debonair man about popping the question. I asked Toni during 'Kum Ba Yah' in the morning assembly song service. It was just one of those crazy, impulsive moments which grips me every few years or so. Or am I changing? Getting busted for swearing has made me less self-conscious, I suppose. Not to mention the fact that the embarrassment and fear of rejection pales in comparison with my terror of the HSC itself. Imminent death motivates people to do the strangest things. And, o yea!, she said yes! But, even so, I'm still not entirely confident. Now I wonder if she *really* likes me, or whether she simply didn't want to hurt my feelings by saying no. I guess I'll never know.

I turn away from the window, but I can still hear the laughter, the shrieking and the mocking, playful threats. The trial exams are over. Study vacation – 'stuvac' – beckons. Doom lurks over the horizon. School is coming to an end.

Today is my last day.

Am I upset? Hell no. I'm glad it's over. I've had enough of Crookwell High. I'm sick of incompetent teachers, two-faced administrators, PE, regulation Windsor knots, morning worship, bitchy cliques, consistently poor grades, lunchtime daydreams and unrequited love. But one final tragic irony remains. As much as I try to avoid it, I cannot help feeling that I am just as much a pretender as those awkward rebels on the field below. I'm a fraud. I cannot escape that fact. I'm the eternal dreamer. I have spent hours every day inside my own mind, hardly ever focusing on the outside world, the harsher reality. And why not? My daydreams this year have been most satisfactory. In them, I have passed all my HSC subjects, won the Egerton-Warburton prize for excellence, solved all the world's philosophical conundrums over lunch with a Monaco bar, patented several scientific inventions and business schemes, written the perfect poem, become rich and famous, given away my accumulated wealth to help less developed countries in Africa, been interviewed by the world's press (whereupon, graciously, I thanked people such as Ms French and Old Ronny for giving me the motivation to rise above rank mediocrity) and, in the process, won the affections of both the most beautiful and intelligent girls in the school.

Today is my last day.

Of course, it would have been nice if some of these things had actually happened. It's terrible having the power to dream of greatness without having the talent (or luck or whatever) to carry it through. But eventually I must awaken and face the music. The day comes for all of us when we will no longer feel particularly special or worthwhile. It's a couple of weeks away yet, but it's coming and I can't do anything about it. On that dawn, I will wake up from the dream, fix myself a nice strong coffee and contemplate the utter meaninglessness of it all. Then I will catch the train and bus to school and sit the exams. A part of me will be lost forever.

I drop the wash-cloth into the bucket by my feet. The window is clean – so clean that I can see my double looking back at me from the field below. The others cannot see it though. They run straight through my reflection. It isn't there.

I should be down there on that field. I have taken a deep personal pride in developing my recalcitrant behaviour this year. As a nihilist-existentialist, defiance comes easy enough. I simply reject anything which doesn't suit my own moral code – in short, everything that goes on in Crookwell High. Yet here I stand in the library, legitimately fulfilling my onerous detention duties. Shouldn't I just blow the final half-hour? Shouldn't I spend my last day at school with the others? No, damn it. I've read about Karl Marx and Vladimir Lenin in Modern History. They were true rebels. They wouldn't have joined in the school Muck-Up Day activities. No, they would have rebelled against them and forged their own distinct Utopias in the library or Russia, or some such phrasing of the *Manifesto of the Communist Party*. Only a true, free-thinking rebel would keep up the fight against the hegemonic incumbent lackey fat cats and power-brokers that constitute the School Board.

Today is my last day.

But soon there won't be a force to rebel against. Our Year will disperse. Another group will take over our mantle as Year Twelves, as we took over the mantle of those that went before us. And so it goes. Forever and ever. Amen.

I have spent six years – over one-third of my life – defining myself against this place – setting myself up as the inverse, the antagonistic counter, the perfect negative to the restrictive, god-fearing regime. What will happen to me once it has gone? What intrinsic meaning will be left for me? Yet what am I thinking? If I'm *lamenting* leaving this school then, truly, I am a fraud.

"It makes you sick, doesn't it?"

What? I had not seen Jennifer Dukes move up to the window beside me. She can't read my thoughts, can she?

"Look at them all. Full of school spirit." Her voice is laced with venom.

Oh yes. The Muck-Up Day activities. But why is Jennifer upset about that? Isn't it her unenviable task – as Year Twelve Student Councillor, the school's top House cheerleader and indisputable head of the Shirleys – to be chock-full of school spirit?

She looks over at me, coolly, expecting me to make some sort of reply.

The answer is so simple that it catches me off-guard. Of course! She is just like me! She, too, has defined herself, and her clique, through the school. Once we leave Year Twelve, her power and status will simply evaporate. This last day means everything to both of us. I'll be a rebel without a cause (just like James Dean I hope) and Jennifer will be a queen without any subjects or empire to speak of.

Jennifer sighs. She is at once powerful (for school still exists), yet vulnerable too. She is a condemned monarch, locked inside her tower, watching the republican hordes dance on the ramparts below. Never before have I seen her look so human.

"Jennifer..." I lower my gaze. "You know something?"

"What?"

"I'm going to miss you, you know."

The effect is magical! She draws her breath back in surprise, her fists clench, her knuckles whiten and, in a supreme Shirleyish moment, her eyes roll back in her head like the spinners in a pokie machine.

"Screw you, you creepy fag."

Ahh, it is a beautiful moment. Just beautiful.

I *am* a fraud.

I'm going to miss this hell-hole.

HIP

Jennifer was well within her rights to call me a creep this afternoon. That's what she calls anyone who doesn't measure up to her standards of hipness. Heck, not that it worries me. I have always been a stylistic void, a hip-free zone. So I guess I *am* a creep. What else do you call someone who wears school socks on 'mufti days' when everyone else is flamboyantly attired? What else do you call someone who wears glasses the size of mine? What else do you call someone who is neither a rugged jock nor academically gifted? 'Creep' just about sums me up. Actually, Jennifer doesn't realise it, but I kind of like the word. I reckon that it has a dark, brooding tone. Being hip like Jennifer is so shallow. I have more depth than that. I'm a creep.

"I'll park here," says Richard, reversing the Frog into a space.

We are outside the shopping centre at Sandhurst. I'm glad that I'm going to the formal hire store with Richard. Last time, for the Year Ten Formal, I came here by myself – and the incompetent sales assistant talked me into wearing a pink suit with black velvet trimmings. Fortunately, I went to that Formal without a date, so I managed to contain the fallout of embarrassment to myself. Needless to say, I've burnt any photos I've come across of the Year Ten Formal. I've learned that there is a fine line between being a creep, and being a bloody idiot.

I feed the parking meter some loose change. There's only a half-hour time limit for this position in peak hour. "We'll have to be quick."

"It won't take us long."

Richard seems pretty relaxed, and that helps me to relax. Richard's not hip, exactly, but he knows what looks good and what doesn't. He always looks cool at school during PE and sport, but I suppose that he has the kind of body that makes anything work. He can wear ripped tee-shirts, baggy trousers, high-cut cross-trainers and various types of caps simultaneously without resembling a complete wally – unlike others I can think of. That's probably why he thinks he'll be able to decide upon a snazzy formal outfit in under thirty minutes. Doubtless, he'll just pick something straight up off the rack. The last time I was here it took me two hours. And even then I couldn't really decide between the pink suit with velvet trim or the aquamarine number with the cream lapels.

Wearing that awful pink suit was not the only time I've come into trouble with clothing fashion at school. Every year Crookwell High has several mufti days, those truly wonderful days in the calendar when students are released from the requirement to wear school uniform, and when creeps such as myself get the chance to show everyone just how hipless we really are. I never knew just how much I liked the bland dress code until that first, fateful mufti day in Year Seven. Before then, I had considered everyone in my year to be as mediocre as the next person. We were a dull, classless microcosm of society. It was nearly impossible to tell the jocks from the nerds from the petrol-heads from the dorks from the hoons from the creeps from the A-crowd. One minute into that mufti day, however, and the once-equal society had disintegrated into its constituent tribes. I discovered that I was a nerd, that Jamie was a dork, that Jennifer was a member of the A-crowd, that Billy was a jock, that Toni came from the upper-middle class of Glendale, and that Greg came from anywhere in Rundle. I hated it. All of a sudden there was another competition to win, a new game to play, a new way of picking winners and losers. That day I swore that I would never play the game again, and when the next mufti day came around I marched proudly into school wearing my grey Crookwell uniform, slightly untucked to demonstrate that I wasn't on the school's side either. My little stand didn't amount to much with the others though. In their eyes, I merely changed from a nerd to a creep.

Richard and I stand in the hire store, perusing the garments on offer.

"Sirs! How are you? Looking for something special?"

Oh god. It's the same dopey assistant who screwed me up two years ago. He saunters over from the cashier. I pretend to look at the item directly in front of me, hoping he'll pass us by. But it just isn't my lucky day.

"An *excellent* choice if I may say so," he fawns.

What? He can't be serious! It is the very same aquamarine outfit with cream lapels that I had forsaken two years ago for all the style and panache of the Pink Horror. Hell, it was this same no-hoper assistant who advised me to do it! He had told me that aquamarine was dead! And I remind him too, in more words or less.

"Sir, I never said that," he protests. "And even if I *did,* well, to say so was very fashionable back then. But now is now and then was then and to re-live the past, however fashionable now, may not be fashionable tomorrow."

"What?"

"Fashion moves in *cycles,* sir. Just try it on. The change rooms are over there." He waves me away and turns to deal with Richard, who I notice to have picked up a more traditional black and white number.

I feel a little put out by the assistant's dismissal, but I go to the change room anyway, hauling the blue nightmare over my shoulder. It is a very cramped room. A full-length mirror is on the back of the door. On the opposite wall, several hooks offer to hang up my school clothes. I may as well try the outfit on, I suppose. If it really is terrible, Richard will be sure to tell me. I start to undress.

While slipping on the pants and fiddling with the gaudy cummerbund, it occurs to me how similar Formals are to school mufti days. A Formal is just another competition really, another fashion parade, albeit on a grander scale. The girls try to outdo each other with the prettiest dresses while the boys go for additional points in the categories of Car-Hiring, Corsages and Cummerbunds. It is rumoured that a couple got expelled several years ago after turning up drunk to the Formal. Apparently, they had availed themselves of the cocktail bar in the hired stretch limo. They went through an entire bottle of spirits on the journey between the girl's house and the school. The fact that they exchanged outfits during the trip didn't go down well with the Board either. I hope Toni and Kim aren't expecting an extravagant limo service to this year's Formal. Richard and I reckon the Frog could do just as good a job at one-millionth of the cost. Sure, we'll do it up a bit for the occasion; make it real special. You have to for the Formal. Girls take the occasion very seriously. They treat it like it's one of Life's ultimate moments. But we don't want to go mental over it. To be frank, I'd prefer a Year Twelve Barbecue instead.

I look in the mirror, fully dressed once more. I'm not sure if the person looking back at me is a creep or a fool. Perhaps Richard will be able to tell. I open the door and move back out into the store.

"So what do you think?"

"*Marvellous!* A real statement, sir. Very hip."

There's that word again: hip. I wonder where it was derived from.

"I was talking to Richard!"

Richard glances at his watch nervously. I notice that he has already tried on his outfit and made his decision. "It'll do."

"You reckon?"

"Yeah. Come on. Let's go."

Well, I suppose that if Richard thinks it looks the goods, then it must be all right. I'm not going to make the same mistake again this year.

"Okay, how much is it?"

The assistant performs some rudimentary mathematics on the back of his pad before blurting out a number about three times higher than I had expected. "But there's a larger deposit on this suit," he explains. "It's still in mint condition. Hardly ever worn. You'll get back the deposit upon its return."

Sure. I return to the change rooms and retrieve my wallet from the hip pocket of my school trousers. Hang on a minute!

Hip. Hip pocket.

Well now I know.

STUVACILLATION

Thursday, Day 1 Stuvac

Thought for today: is it just me, or does everything suddenly become more interesting when I have to study for exams? The quality of television programming, in particular, has lifted several notches from last week – as if cunning network bosses deliberately target the HSC-suffering sixteen to nineteen year old panic-stricken demographic. Why else would they bring back re-runs of *Family Ties* to a regular afternoon timeslot? Or schedule a two week retrospective, *Home and Away: The Early Years,* commemorating the anniversary of my favourite soapy drama?

Some people can handle locking themselves away from the outside world for 336 hours, scribbling arcane notes about the BOP or CAD, dreaming about nothing else but the Sine Rule or binomial expansions, and only stopping occasionally for food, sleep or the obligatory toilet break.

I cannot.

I need noise to study. I need to hear life going on around me. My mind has to be massaged with media other than the foolscap pages on my desk. It wants to be free. It wants me to go outside and lie in the sun. It wants to sleep. It wants to write about anything other than vectors or Emily Dickinson. Christ! Stuvac is going to be hell: two weeks of recollection, revision, memorisation and mental disintegration.

I looked at my school bag, bursting with large subject folders. I pondered my options. I went back to bed.

Friday, Day 2 Stuvac

Thirteen days to go before my first exam. Had a major panic attack. I'm so underprepared! Watched a program on lead poisoning to cheer myself up. Realising that I had procrastinated only triggered a second panic attack at four o'clock.

Saturday, Day 3 Stuvac

Thank god for the weekend! Thought about Greg. What a terrible thing to be constrained from studying on the Sabbath day! Or having to attend church for that matter. Listened to some of my favourite tapes in my room. Mum thought I was listening to my stress tapes from Dr Newth. She doesn't know I use alcohol now.

Sunday, Day 4 Stuvac

Have come to the conclusion that I need a well-defined plan to meet my study requirements – and to prevent me from further time-wasting. Phoned up Richard to check his progress. He has already covered Economics! Panic attack. Watched an interesting story about synchronised swimming on *World Sports.* Mulled over an outline of a draft plan during the Sunday night movie.

Monday, Day 5 Stuvac

Felt strange. Lay in bed debating my options with myself until eleven o'clock. Settled on my preliminary draft plan outline by two o'clock, after surveying my key subject areas:

Days Remaining: 9
Subjects to Study: 6, 5:   English 2U
                              Maths 2U
                              Economics 2U

Modern History 2U

~~Biology 2U~~

Physics 2U

Have decided to make rote-learnable notes for all my subjects, but with two ingenious twists: (a) as English is my first exam, I will study and memorise in reverse exam order to avoid studying English twice, and (b) as I will be assessed upon only ten units, I can afford to drop one subject entirely and concentrate my efforts on the remaining five – bye-bye Biology. Satisfied with my day's work.

Home and Away (HAA): Classic episode with Bobbie and Frank. Meanwhile, Alf is a hard man to please.

Tuesday, Day 6 Stuvac

Have discovered a three day window in my exam timetable between Biology and Physics. Will study Physics in that window instead of now. This is extremely fortuitous. Now I have eight days to study four subjects. This leaves exactly two days per subject – one day for preparing rote-learnable notes, and one day for memorising them. Rote-learning at a rate of three pages an hour means that I must limit my notes to approximately fifteen foolscap sheets.

Modern History. Have categorised my material into six core areas: Causes of World War I (two pages), World War I (three pages), Home Front (two pages), Germany 1918-1939 (four pages), World War II (three pages), plus Why Stalin was Good for the Soviet Union (one page – I'm banking on my essay appearing in the Twentieth-Century Russia section).

Family Ties (FT): Jennifer upsets a friend but they make up in the end.

HAA: Alf blames Ailsa for a break-in at the shop. Carly looks confused.

Wednesday, Day 7 Stuvac

A more relaxing day. Listened to my 'positive thinking' tapes from Dr Newth. Then settled in the living room with my History notes and a cup of coffee. Trimmed the number of points I made on Causes of World War I (as it was tested last year). Fell asleep on the couch.

Thursday, Day 8 Stuvac

Panic attack. One week to go until my first exam. Had a phone call from Greg. He told me that he has studied everything but Biology. Asked if I had looked at it yet. Said no. Hung up. Made note to kill Greg.

Economics. Divided subject into eight core topics of two pages each: fiscal policy, monetary policy, wages policy, micro-economic reform, the external economy, employment, inflation, and the economics of less developed countries. Based on an informal analysis of six former HSC Economics papers, as well as contemporary issues, I have targeted the current account deficit for the compulsory question. Will study Toni's essay that was photocopied by Mr White for the rest of the class. Toni would do well to memorise it herself.

FT: Mrs Keaton upsets Alex, but they smooth over their differences in the end.

HAA: Carly struggles with her own exam study. She takes to using No Doze caffeine tablets. I prefer the real thing myself.

Friday, Day 9 Stuvac

Sunny day, so took to the driveway to memorise my Eco notes. They make little sense, but as long as I remember the string of points coupled with the appropriate linking sentences I should be okay. Furthermore, I will be able to toss in my 'Level of Economic Activity' (income – expenditure – demand – production – investment – employment – income) diagrams into every core area. Finding it hard to memorise my economic indicator statistics, however. I keep mixing up the numbers for inflation with unemployment.

FT: Mr Keaton upsets Mrs Keaton but, with the combined help of Alex, Mallory and Jennifer, they make up in the end.

HAA: Bobbie and Frank argue. Ailsa is upset with Alf. Carly conceals her No Doze caffeine tablets from Deputy Principal Fisher.

Saturday, Day 10 Stuvac

Slept in as a reward for remembering most of my Eco notes last night. Greg probably has to go on a nature walk for Sabbath School. Sucker! Talked with Richard over the phone for three hours about girls. Made me think about Toni. I wonder if she's expecting me to make any moves after the Formal.

Maths: Chose not to use the same studying technique as applied to my other subjects. Instead, I did hundreds of tedious questions from my Goodman mathematics textbook. Jeez, Goodman's books are poorly laid out. I could hardly read them. He could do with a decent desktop publishing program. Finished calculus and geometry by midnight and went to bed.

Sunday, Day 11 Stuvac

Dad thought I needed a break from my rigorous routine. Played a game of tennis for the first time in three years. After a few games I managed to hit the ball. Came back home to find *The Wackiest Ship in the Navy* on the box, followed by *Get Smart.* Had to watch both. Considered hitting the trigonometry revision but thought better of it – may as well take the whole day off now. Enjoyed the elusive wit of Jacko in Chapter Eight of his ripper autobiography, subtitled 'Larrikin on Tour'.

Monday, Day 12 Stuvac

Another panic attack. Only two days before my first exam, English, and I haven't even started studying for it yet! My redrafted study draft should have been redrafted earlier to save me the stress. Had a hot brandy to calm the nerves before pulling out my English folders. Disregarded Ms French's dictations immediately, but kept her photocopied essays by high-profile critics. Decided upon *Brodie's Notes* as my major source. After examining the last few English HSC papers, I have decided that there cannot be two compulsory poetry questions this time around. Dropped Dickinson and kept Slessor.

FT: Alex sells out on a friend but makes up in the end.

HAA: Ailsa is still estranged from Alf. Carly agonises over the No Doze tablets.

Tuesday, Day 13 Stuvac

I am a complete nervous wreck. Not even Dr Newth's tapes and endless repetitions of 'Don't Worry, Be Happy' on my Walkman can help me. Took two of Mum's valiums to alleviate the nausea. Slept. Woke up. Tried memorising my *Othello* notes on the driveway, pacing between the garage doors and the letterbox. Some schoolkids from up the road made fun of my stress headband, ugg-boots and striped pyjamas. Went inside. Had an early tea. Tried to cover some drama notes, but for some bizarre reason my mind filled with images of death and the Nazi Third Reich. I think my Modern History notes are seeping out of my brain. Decided to rest my head with some television.

FT: Mallory betrays Skippy but makes up in the end.

HAA: Fisher comes across Carly's No Doze tablets in a snap locker search. Frank gives Bobbie a look. Alf contemplates purchasing a burglar alarm.

Midnight: Given up all hope. Resigned to defeat. Going to bed. My first exam is only nine hours away. Thought about Richard, Greg, Kim and Toni. God! Does she like me? What should I do? I can't tell her that I love her. I can't reveal those sorts of feelings. It could ruin everything. We have a pretty good thing going at the moment. Saying that I love her would put it all at risk. If she doesn't return my love, I'd be too ashamed of myself ever to see her again.

Now it's time to sleep. Time to dream. I wish classes were still on. I hate endings. It's all so terribly final.

I don't want to see the dawn. I really don't.

Why can't it stay away forever?

Postscript

They drive away together.

It's a green Torana. An early model. Mag wheels though. Twin exhaust. Tinted windows. The driver taps the steering wheel in rhythm to Dead Bone *on the car stereo. The girl in the front seat adjusts the air-conditioning. One of the passengers in the back seat remembers that he hasn't put on his seatbelt. The other stares out through the window. They are together, but each is caught up in their own thoughts. After years of study, it has come down to this. Today. The post office. The results.* Dead Bone *grinds on.*

The other turns back towards him. She takes a dollar from her purse. It feels cold against her palm.

"What are you doing?" he asks.

"It's a predictive experiment."

"What?"

"Don't you remember?"

He nods his head. "You were right. It was a dumb experiment. Forget it."

"Don't you want to predict the future any more?"

"Not really."

"Why?"

"I don't think I want to know about it. I'd prefer just to let it happen. I'll find out soon enough when the post office opens." His brow furrows. "Besides, you said that it was impossible to predict real outcomes with a coin."

The other places the dollar upon her thumb. "Perhaps I was wrong about that. There is always the chance that I could be wrong."

"What are you two talking about?" The driver glances up into the rear-view mirror.

He leans forward in his seat. "She's going to predict whether I'm going to pass or fail the HSC."

"How the hell is she going to do that?"

"With a coin."

140

The driver agrees. "It's a little fifty-fifty for me too, man." He turns the car on to the main road towards the centre of Sandhurst.

"Well, we could predict yours at the same time then," says the other.

The girl in the front seat is unconvinced. "Whether we pass or fail is not the issue. It's whether we get into our choice of university course that really counts. I'll look at the Admissions card first, then my TER."

"Weren't you going to Harvey College regardless?" queries the driver.

"Maybe." A cold silence.

"Anyway, the coin is only a two-way predictor," says one of the back-seat passengers.

"Two sides, two possibilities, right?" says the other.

"Right. It's got to be either pass or fail."

"Well, are you two going to talk about it forever or are you going to do it?"

The other nods. She has the coin ready to toss. "Heads is pass. Tails fails."

He tenses up beside her as she spins the coin. There are so many possibilities really. He could fail while the others pass, or vice versa, or some other combination of pass-fail could arise between them all. The simple coin test is a little crude for this particular experiment. He needs another hypothesis to test – a proper two-way outcome. She is so close to him. He can smell her perfume. Could she love him? The coin hangs in the air. He makes his decision.

"Heads!"

"So are we going to pass then?" asks the driver.

"Well... I'm fifty percent sure. I'll toss again."

The dollar is spinning madly once more. It hits the roof of the car and bounces into her lap. He gulps in surprise.

"Heads again. Seventy-five percent certain now."

"Hey! This is great," says the driver. "Keep it up."

"But it can't last," says the girl in the front. "The chances of continually getting heads must be really small. Every time you toss a head, you only move closer to tossing a tail later on."

"No you don't," corrects the other, holding the coin in her hand. "Every toss is still always a fifty-fifty chance. It doesn't matter what came up before."

She tosses it again. Another head. Again. Another head. Fifth time. Head.

The boy shakes his head in disbelief. How certain should he be before he decides to act?   There are arguments raging, voices clamouring to be heard: Life isn't decided for us by a supreme being you know... But what do I know...?   I can't tell her that I love her... I will be a laughing stock...! Toni isn't interested in my type at all... I'm a creep... geeks, dags, fags... Screw you, you creepy fag... dykes, dweebs, losers... Only nerdy turds get into the Council... If it's any consolation, I voted for you... That's life for you, I suppose... And to think that I thought you were cool... You've just got to learn to be cool, that's all... Why can't people see beyond the surface...?   And is this really the truth anyway...?   Heck, there's no absolute right or wrong... Toni?   And me...?   There's so much to do before my time at Crookwell comes to an end... Now I'm young and awfully vibrant... True, I'm known to some of them as the Black Vortex of Despair... But some day I won't be... Some day I'll prove them wrong about me... I wish I could relax... Hell, we were all innocent at one time or another... Nobody really cares. You shouldn't be so self-conscious... It's nothing to be worried about... Come on, Gary. Let's go. You only live once... Here's your big moment, Gary... Do it now, Gary... Go to her...

"How certain are you now?" he asks the other.

"Well, let's see... I make it over ninety-five percent certain."

That's enough. He closes his eyes and kisses her softly on the cheek.

"What was that for?" *She is surprised.*

The car shudders to a halt beside the post office.

The music stops.

"I... I was almost certain that it was what I should do. Sorry." *He backs away, embarrassed.*

The driver opens his door and gets out. So does the girl from the front seat. They stand together by the front of the green car. The sun beats down. It is a quarter past eight. The post office is still closed. Several others are already waiting by the front door. Some smoke. Some sit and talk with their friends. Others just sit, silent. Some are from Crookwell High, but most are not. A few stand beside their parents. Everyone is nervous. The post office opens in fifteen minutes.

"Hey! Come on you two. Get out of my car."

The tinted back window rolls down. She holds her arm out and drops the dollar into the driver's hand. "Uh. We'll wait in here. Can you get me a drink?   Thanks. Sorry?   Oh. Make it a Monaco bar instead." *The window rolls back up again.*

The driver looks down at the coin in his hand.
Heads again!
He turns it over.